Departed Death

By Robbie Michael

Since 2020

This book is dedicated to you. Yep, this is for the reader. You're holding my book and reading it! I think that's awesome.

Wait! Does this mean you can now say you've had a book dedicated to you?

Table of Contents

1

I'm an evil person. Why would a loving God choose to love me?

Tears fell down the young woman's face as she stared up at the sky as if looking toward heaven. The stars were winking in and out with each cloud that crossed its surface. The moon's rays shone so brightly that it illuminated the passing clouds. A light breeze cruised through the streets, its presence ineffective to the passers-by. She sat there taking it all in, crying out in her thoughts, but she felt nothing but shame.

Tonight, a church was the center of activity here. Its Gothic architecture and iron picket fencing pronounced its differences from the colony of buildings in the street. The doors, thrown wide open, revealed an aisle that led straight to a modest altar. People trooped into the church without order. The only code required to get in, the only code everyone who stepped on the stairs leading in adhered to was that of reverent silence. The young woman longed to feel what they were feeling. The smiles, their demeanor said they were happy to be at church. She walked towards the church, hoping to feel the warmth everyone else seemed to feel.

Across the church's front was a tree line resembling a protective barrier between the road in front and its field. Outside the treeline were shadows clinging to the trees giving it the tincture of the ominous – the fencing of hell, the land of darkness – as opposed to the inviting church with all the beautiful golden light pouring out its doors and windows.

The young woman walked out of the trees' shadows, moved into the street, and stopped at the curb just outside the church. She moved closer then stopped abruptly, her movements not unlike a vehicle jerking from a faulty engine. She stepped into the light, revealing her dark hair falling across her shoulders in curly locks. Her eyes were almond-shaped, dark, and filled with a suppressed hunger and curiosity, one that increased in intensity as she continued to stare at the church's entrance. The woman watched the church's entrance for a little longer before walking through its gates. However, rather than ply the path through the church's doors, she took a turn towards the church's parking lot and sat gently on one of the benches there. Then she leaned into the backrest and watched the people going into the church with sorrow and envy.

I should be there with them, the young woman thought. *Why do I do this to myself? Why continue to torture myself? This is my punishment. This is hallowed ground, and nothing about me is holy.*

Tears streamed down her eyes once more, tears that were as lonely and pain-filled as the feelings in her chest. They slithered across her face and dropped onto her denim pants, creating dark blotches on the sky-blue fabric.

"I'm sorry, God," she whispered. "Please help me—" her voice caught in her throat.

I'm an evil person. He won't listen to me. Why would he?

Just then, she felt a buzzing sensation against her left thigh. She sniffed, wiped the sleeve of her black turtleneck top across her face, then dug her phone out of her pant's pocket. It was Jeffrey. She got to her feet and answered the phone.

"Savannah, where are you?"

"Dude, chill. I'm on my way," she replied. "I had to make a quick stop. We've got plenty of time."

"Okay, but I want to get there a few minutes early," Jeffrey said. "I like to—"

"Yeah, I got it! You like to be early," Savannah interrupted. "I said I'm on my way."

Savannah hung up the phone, stared at the church for a while longer, then turned and walked more boldly and quickly than when she'd come in. It was time to go to work.

***

Henry and Madilyn Sawyer. Both of them were in their 40's, full of hope and promise of a bright future. They were bathed in auras – a light foggy shine that glowed from their entire bodies – and had corresponding dates hanging over their heads. There was a difference to the woman's aura that puzzled Savannah. Hers was slightly brighter than her husband's. It was something that Savannah had never seen before, not like this.

Nevertheless, they were happy and oblivious, as most people like them were. Savannah watched them walk out of their duplex through the windshield of Jeffrey's Audi A7. The couple strolled down the driveway to their SUV, which they'd left idling at the entrance. Everything had happened just as the file on Savannah's lap said it would. They'd driven a few miles away from home, only to return. They had forgotten something.

Now, Savannah watched with chagrin because she knew there was no way the couple could escape what was coming to them. Deep down in her chest, there was a throbbing agitation, something more like defiance in knowing she couldn't help. She had to suppress her feelings to keep from getting in trouble. She had a job to do.

There was a slight stagger to the man's walk, almost invisible, and could only be made out by very attentive eyes, which was all Savannah and her handler, Jeffrey, could be at this point. Savannah glanced at Jeffrey and studied him. Is he someone she could trust? He sat in the driver's seat with his face plastered in indifference and bent over a sketchpad on which he diligently worked. That indifference she could understand. They had to do a job, and it was often better to get through it with a straight face than one crumpled up in complaint. Whenever Jeffrey accompanied her on missions, her biggest bother was whether his heart was as steely as his face. She turned back to the couple – the reason why they'd been sitting attentively in the car for two straight hours.

The man and his wife walked over to the other side of the car, then he opened the door and held it open for his wife. Madilyn, a head shorter than her husband, smiled and stretched to give him a peck on the lips. Savannah did not fail to notice the simple luxury in the way they dressed. Henry was in a two-piece suit, while Madilyn was in a flowing wine-red sleeveless satin gown.

They sure are dressed a little nice for a couple going on a date, Savannah thought.

She flipped open the ink-black dossier sitting on her lap and leafed through two papers before landing on the one she was looking for. Her eyes skimmed through most of the details until she got to the part where the target's intended destination was listed. She felt dread overtake her, wrapping her up like a blanket. She flicked her eyes back to the couple.

Oh, no.

They were on their way to a gala event where they planned to raise money for a local women's shelter.

No, not again. They don't deserve this.

"Do you ever wonder why they have to go through this?" she asked as she turned to Jeffrey. "I mean, they're going to a freaking gala to raise money for a battered women's shelter. And can you see her aura? It's different. She's not like most people. This isn't right!"

Savannah slammed the flat of her palm on the dashboard, releasing her pent-up frustration.

"This job is getting increasingly difficult. It's like each mission I complete pushes me to another level of hardness. You know, I've lost count of just how many people I've watched die. Unfairly, I might add! Is that even normal? Seriously, nobody should get to see that much death, and I think it's getting to me."

Jeffrey's hands stopped moving. He straightened up, turned his face from his sketching, and donned a shrewd expression for Savannah. A few missions with Jeffrey had taught her what that look meant – it was time to shut up and keep quiet about whatever misgivings were locked up inside. Savannah looked away after holding Jeffrey's gaze for a second. Jeffery pressed his lips together until they formed a hard line, then he went back to sketching. He'd made a few quick strokes before he paused, giving an audible heavy sigh.

"Savannah, you know I think you're an okay person, right," he asked in the manner of someone who had a terrible taste in their mouth.

"Wow," Savannah exclaimed, her head moving backward for effect. "Just okay?"

"Look, I usually do this alone. It's better that way. It makes the mission efficient and quick. Why the rest of us suddenly have to babysit you is beyond me. I like being alone, always alone, and *in silence*. I bring my sketch pad, and I draw. It's my way of dealing with the silence. I look at it like it's my me time, and I like it that way."

He held up his pad and pushed its open page towards her.

"Today, I am drawing in graffiti style. It's kind of my go-to. I have 32 of these drawings. 32. Do you know why 32?"

Savannah opened her mouth to answer, but Jeffrey held up his hand, cutting her off. Then he continued.

"I've been on 32 of these jobs. That's 32 jobs watching people die. I'm okay with that; it's what we do. We have a gift – if you want to call it that. Then I go home, read a comic or two, watch a little TV, and I go to sleep. I sleep well too. Wanna know why? Because I find a way to cope. These simple little sketches might not look like much to you, but they help me cope. It would be best if you found your thing. Besides, what're you going to do? Go to war with all of us and save everyone?" He laughed, then leaned into his pad and began sketching again. "Oh, that would be the day, wouldn't it? Little ol' Savannah, Mr. Garner's favorite, fighting all of us. Now, that's funny!" He regained his composure and continued, "I would like to draw in silence, please. I assume you know what that is."

Jeffrey's reaction was as good a reason as any for why both of them weren't the perfect partners. Not only did he not like the deferential treatment she got from the boss, Mr. Garner, but he also disliked her consistent questions regarding the nature of their job. Jeffrey couldn't help but wonder how Savannah landed a job with the firm in the first place. An uncomfortable silence crept into the car, only to be broken the next second.

"But think about it," Savannah said in the same manner as she would if she were speaking to herself.

Jeffery scoffed, dropped the pencil on the sketch pad, and raised his head.

"Those people are good people," Savannah continued, "like, really good people. You saw the file. What if we could save them? There are kids in that car. What about…"

The words fell out of her mouth at the same time that her face shone with exciting surprise. Something extraordinary had happened as she watched the couple take a left at the traffic stop ahead.

"What's that look for," Jefferey asked, his brows furrowed. "Hey, don't go off getting any wild ideas."

"Look. The woman. Her date changed. It's not today anymore. Something changed. That has to mean something. I told you her aura was different!"

The lines on his forehead deepened.

"What's this thing about dates changing and auras," he asked. What do you mean it's changed? You're not getting out of this job, Savannah. That couple is scheduled to die today. The date doesn't change, Savannah, because you suddenly have a conscience. That's not how it works. Everything needed for the execution of this mission is right there in the dossier. We complete the task."

With fixated eyes, Savannah stared straight ahead without any indication she was listening to Jeffrey.

"Hey, I don't mean to be so harsh. Are you okay," he asked. "You're making me a little uncomfortable. Someone had to tell you what we're all thinking. Okay, I'll bite. What do you mean by the date changing? And what do you mean, her aura? You're not one of those freaky palm reading psychos, are you? That sure would answer a lot of questions for the rest of us."

"Yes, this has happened before with the date. Not with the aura, though. It just sucks. That's all I am saying. It would be different if the couple were, I don't know, mass murderers or something. I just find it odd that nobody asks the questions I do. Why them? Why those kids? Something within is screaming out that none of this is right."

Jeffrey started to speak but didn't know what to say. His head became crowded with a lot of questions. There was this tincture of mystery that Savannah carried with her. It usually sparked Jeffrey's curiosity. However, today's version with the dates and aura furnished the intensity of that curiosity, and he would have given in to it were it not for the sudden beeping that filled the air inside the car. His eyes flew to his wristwatch. Then he snapped his sketch pad close and tossed it towards the back.

"It's time," he said.

Savannah felt a bitter sense of disgust at the thought of what was going to happen next.

They didn't need to drive too far to find what they were looking for. As Savannah and Jeffrey came up around a bend, they were confronted with the sight of an upturned SUV lying by the side of the road, its frame twisted, taillights and headlights glaring, and a million shards of glass across the street. The dust and smoke still filled the air surrounding the vehicle. Jeffrey let their car idle just off the road about 200 feet behind the carnage, then he and Savannah walked towards the scene.

Savannah felt a burning in her chest like her heart was being held above a spit, slowly roasting. She saw a small amount of blood flowing out of where the passenger window used to be, and then her eyes fell on the source – the couple they'd been watching. They hung off their seats by their seatbelts. They were both unconscious but still alive, although their auras were a lot fainter than before. Suddenly, the woman's aura began to glimmer brighter. Savannah watched Jeffrey move with a sense of purpose, and she knew she could do nothing to help anyone in the vehicle.

Jeffrey picked up a long shard of glass from the broken windscreen. He crouched close to the woman and drove the shard into her neck, thus staging everything to look like an accident through and through. Savannah felt waves of uneasiness roll through her body. Oddly, though, there was a sparkle of admiration for the simplicity of Jeffrey's execution. He carried the whole thing out clinically.

I'm an evil person, Savannah thought. *What's wrong with me?*

Jeffrey stepped back from the upturned SUV with a sigh and watched it with the pride of an artisan admiring his work. He pulled out his phone and took a picture.

"Flawless. Okay, let's bail," Jeffrey said with a smile. "These souls have just been reaped."

Savannah felt a flare of pain in her chest, but she gave Jeffrey a small smile in honor of his comment. She looked at the SUV one more time.

If only I hadn't been left in the dark about this, thought Savannah. *Maybe I could have done more.*

Savannah and Jeffrey turned, got back into the black car, and drove off.

2

The bustle of the city that never sleeps filtered in the windows to Savannah's two-bedroom apartment. New York City's liveliness and excitement weren't even powerful enough to staunch the sullenness that filled the atmosphere in the apartment. For Savannah, the sound of a million people was torture to her ears at that moment.

They'll all die anyway, she thought. *Whether they are innocent or not doesn't matter. If I don't do it, then someone else will come along and do it. If it's my job, then why do I feel so dirty?*

She staggered towards the windows, her bathrobe flailing around her legs, a half-empty bottle of tequila in her hand – its contents sloshing vigorously -- and drew the blinds over the windows, shutting off the intruding sound entirely. She walked back to her living room and plopped onto the couch. The depression of her weight upset an empty bottle of tequila lying on the couch, causing it to roll off onto the brown woolen rug on the ground.

Not even the bottom of this bottle can make the pain go away. At least it helps me sleep.

With her back against the couch's headrest, Savannah gazed at the ceiling, her blank eyes seeing everything and nothing. Her mind was replete with thoughts of displeasure and regret, and at the forefront was the face of the woman she'd watch Jeffery terminate.

I could have saved them, she thought. *I could have saved that family like I did the others. I've gotten quite good at it. It wouldn't have been that hard, but apparently, I need a babysitter.*

Having someone keep watch over Savannah was a new development. It was the third mission she was executing as a paired partner. And like the two before now, she'd been helpless to save the victims selected for death. This opened a new angle of consideration. *What if the boss assigned these missions on purpose because he's onto me?*

The thought sent jolts of fear through her body. She'd never seen the boss, but she knew his reputation. Rogue employees had a way of disappearing if they didn't abide by the company rules. There was something that reeked of the ominous whenever the boss's name or the thought of him came up. Her eyes carelessly roved the entire place and fell on a framed letter sitting on the shelf. The letter came in from her boss on the day she sealed her employment with his firm. That was some years ago. At the time, she'd thought it ridiculous that the boss would send her a framed letter of his appreciation. Now, the more she stared at the letter, the greater her anger burned. The framed letter was a reminder, a taunting one, that she'd sold her conscience and her humanity for money.

Like water in a kettle when it hit its boiling point, Savannah yelled. Simultaneously, she grabbed the empty bottle of tequila on the floor and flung it towards the framed letter. The bottle hit the edge of the shelf instead, glanced towards the wall, and broke on impact. Savannah's face grimaced as her soul was bathed with the tepid catharsis of her rage. She pulled her knees close to her chest, and then she wrapped her hands around them. Her shoulders shook as high-pitched sobs lanced the quiet of her apartment.

After a few moments, Savannah quietened. She sniffed and brought up her head, shaking a few strands of hair from her vision. She put her lips to the top of the bottle, then she tipped it up and guzzled from it, stopping only when it was near empty. She winced as she felt its burning sensation flowing down her tongue and throat. Suddenly, she felt this new rush of bravado, flushing out much of the trepidation that had clouded her mind moments ago.

Whatever's going to happen is totally worth it, she thought. *Why continue to fight it?*

In truth, she could not see her future continuing with the firm; she knew it eventually had to end. Too much was happening, and she was getting crushed under the weight of it all. But this in itself presented a catch-22 situation. Getting employed in the firm was a straight ride to hell. It was a commitment one made for their entire life. And in recognition of that, the firm paid its staff exceedingly well. However, for Savannah, it was no longer about the money. Families like the one that had just died were worth more than any amount she would receive.

Savannah stood to her feet and would have fallen over the table in front of her had she not gripped the edge of it at the very last minute. She stayed that way for a few moments, trying to collect herself before moving into the bathroom. She'd already prepared a bath in the tub. So, she let her bathrobe slip off her body, crumpling on the cold floor. Gingerly, Savannah got into the tub, feeling the warmth of the water spread over her skin. She put on folk music and raised the volume on her speaker so it could drown out everything, forming the first layer for the world she was about to escape to. Then she sank deeper into the bath until only her nose and mouth jutted out of the surface of the water.

***

Many miles away, close to Little Neck Bay, a group of three people sat around a drum of fire just outside a big mansion. Surrounded by a thicket of tall woods, it was difficult for the moon's rays to access the location, except when it hung overhead.

The flame from the drum burned steadily, producing a warm orange glow that illuminated the faces of the people around. There was an older man continually puffing on a pipe. He appeared to be deep in thought. Other than the occasional whisper to himself, he remained quiet. A tall younger man with a round face and hazel eyes glowed from the fire's reflection. He leaned back in his chair and stared at the night sky. Lastly, a woman with short spiky brown hair sat across from the two men. She maintained a stern look on her face as she poked at the fire.

"Teacher," the woman called, "I don't know how you can smoke on that thing."

"That's one thing I haven't been able to wrap my head around since we became a team," the young man said with a faint British accent. "You'd think as an old man, he'd consider his health, eh?"

The older man stared straight ahead and let out a raspy chuckle. He puffed on the pipe for a while before withdrawing it from his lips.

"I'm fairly certain," he said, his voice crackly, drawn-out like a breath, "that you both know something about tradition, even if it's just an inkling."

"Tradition," the young man questioned with a strain of amusement to his tone. "Don't you mean habit?"

Isla stared at the old man, her expression showing her agreement with the young man.

"This is more of a tradition. My father also liked to enjoy a pipe when he was deep in thought. I find this relaxing, and it helps me to focus. You can call it a habit if you want to." The young man began to speak, but the old man cut him off. "Before you speak, Oliver, remember that I've been doing this line of work longer than you've been alive. I know more about the inner workings of life than you do. Life is far too complex. So, if I choose to indulge in this one thing, I shall do so without judgment."

"Well, maybe you can teach me the ways of smoking a pipe. I always thought I would be more of a cigar man. What're you deep in thought about? Is it about—"

"Her? Yeah, just trying to wrap my mind around everything. Obviously, something has changed. Life has a strange way of working itself out. How do you explain the matter of The Chosen One working for whom she was born to fight against?"

Except for the crackling of the fire, no one else said a word for some time.

After a while, Oliver asked, "Don't you think we've watched her long enough? Can't we just move in? We don't even know if she will listen to us. What do you think, Isla?"

"Teacher, I fear that we have to think about the worst-case scenario," the young woman said. "It's only a matter of time before she goes too far and can't be redeemed. What do we do then?"

"Yes, I know," Teacher said. "Indeed, you're both right. We've watched enough. If we're to reach out to her, we have to do it now. I've been praying. Mr. Garner is on to something. I just don't think he knows what it is yet."

"We can't let him get to her," Isla stated. "Otherwise, all this, all the time we've given to the cause, will be for nothing. We've sacrificed everything."

"Calm yourself, Isla," Teacher replied.

"Umf! Look at me. I'm *relaxing* near a fire. How much more relaxed can I get?"

"If you lie down, perhaps? Off you pop," Oliver quipped.

Isla stared daggers at him.

"Woah," Oliver said, flinging his arms up in surrender.

Isla turned to Teacher.

"What now?" she asked him.

"What now?" A small smile adorned his wrinkled face. "Well, for starters, I guess an introduction to our dear Savannah is in order."

***

Savannah emerged from the tub, having spent almost an hour underneath the water. She toweled herself, put on her bathrobe, and walked out of the bathroom. The sound of folk music still filled the air, but she wasn't interested anymore. Even underwater, she couldn't get the images of the people she'd done jobs on out of her head. As time went on, these images continued to bombard her mind more and more. They were her burden to bear, an instinctive response to all the things she'd done. Savannah did not think there was ever a coping mechanism that could help alleviate the weight of guilt she carried in her chest, a weight she felt grow heavier with each mission she completed. Savannah often wondered if there would be a moment when the weight became too much.

There was a slight sway in her steps as she moved. The effects of her binge-drinking hadn't completely worn off. If anything, the hot bath seemed to accelerate the effects the alcohol had on her. Any other time this would have been the moment she stopped. Savannah usually knew her limits, and she was flirting with that line tonight. She stopped by the table to have another drink, deciding she could at least use a glass instead of guzzling every drop she could get from the bottle. She poured herself a drink, stopping only when the glass was nearly overflowing. She picked it up gingerly, leaning forward to avoid any spilling on her, and took a large gulp.

Have I gone too far, Savannah wondered as she let out a heavy sigh. *Has the weight become too heavy?*

She walked into her bedroom, then over to her shelf and slid it aside, revealing a small wooden panel in the wall. Savannah slid the panel to the left, uncovering a small chamber filled with photos. Savannah felt a flush of happiness that revealed itself as a smile on her face. The glum look she had carried through to this point was quickly becoming a wisp. She tilted her glass as a toast to the people in the pictures.

The pictures in the chamber belonged to people she had saved, people who she'd been given missions on but was able to save, given that the assigned case was hers to execute alone. The smile on her face widened as she thought of the happy lives they would be leading under the secret identities she'd given them. Savannah made it a point of duty to assign new locations and identities to the people she saved. Then she bought bodies from the morgue and used them as proof of an accomplished mission. In the miserable life she currently led, these were her only source of happiness. Saving these families was her way of balancing the scales.

Suddenly, Savannah whipped her head towards her door. She thought she'd heard something. She didn't have to wait long for clarification; she heard it again. It was the sound of her doorbell. This startled her since very few people knew where she lived. Quickly, she threw off her bathrobe and jumped into her pajamas, and then she hurried out.

As she exited her room, Savannah frowned. The doorbell was ringing incessantly. If this were an emergency and had been someone from work, they would have found a way to enter.

Whoever's at that door is either on crack, is pissed, or is scared, she thought, hoping it was the first.

She paused as soon as she got to the door. She stooped close and gazed through the peephole. She pulled her head back immediately as though someone had tried to poke her eye with a stick. Her face creased with a frown, and she peered through it again in disbelief. When she withdrew her face, the frown had morphed into concern.

"No, no, no," Savannah said as she stood to her feet. She stalked away from the door, turned, and raked her fingers through her hair. "You're not supposed to be here," she said with a quiver to her voice. The ringing was still going on, as constant as ever.

Savannah stared at the door for a second. Then she moved to it, pulled the bolts back, and opened the door to reveal an older man in a rumpled shirt. His messy hair and equally disturbed face let her immediately know that something was wrong.

"Glen," Savannah said, acknowledging his presence.

Glen and his wife were one of the first families she'd saved from death. She made sure to set them up with new identities and sent them out to Montana. Their case always stuck out because she was convinced it was too sloppy. Yet, nobody found out. The deal she made with Glen and his wife was reasonably straightforward. Once they left, they were never to show their faces again if they wanted to live out the rest of their lives in peace. She stressed that the bounty on their lives would be forfeited as long as they stayed in Montana. Savannah stared at Glen for a moment, trying to figure out why he would be here. The bags under his eyes, the tear stains on his face, and the overall disheveled look almost confirmed her biggest fear.

"You're not supposed to be here. I thought I made this perfectly clear. Someone could see you. Quick, come inside," Savannah beckoned quickly with her arm, ushering him inside with haste.

"You look…" she began to say, but Glen caught her off.

"You liar," Glen growled.

Savannah leaned backward, stunned by Glen's outburst. He continued to talk like he didn't notice.

"You said we were safe," Glen yelled angrily. "They know everything. Th-they found us. Why is this happening? What did we do? Oh, God! She's gone!"

While Savannah was still reeling from his outburst, trying to make sense of everything he'd just said, Glen thrust his phone in her face. With her confused eyes still trained on his face, Savannah took the phone from Glen's hand. She looked at its screen, and her heart began to thump so hard she could hear it in her ears. The photo on the screen displayed a wall with something written in red paint.

Is that blood? She asked herself. *Please don't let it be blood.*

However, the words on the wall contained an unrestrained venom that seemed only to answer the question in her heart, and she didn't like it.

The words were in bold legible letters: **You are next.**

"Who wrote this?" Savannah asked, looking up. "Why did they write this? What happened?"

Tears were rolling down Glen's face now, an endless stream of them. The fiery rage he'd come in with had drained from his being, leaving behind a flushed pallor.

"What happened, Glen?"

Savannah's voice carried her confusion and rising fear.

"Scroll through to the rest of the pictures," Glen said.

Savannah did, and a tiny yelp escaped her mouth as her eyes spread wide open in horror. The next photo featured additional details to the wall with the red painting. Barb was lying on the ground underneath the message on the wall. The line of crimson red across her throat connected to a pool of blood beside her. Savannah felt her heart go aflame with so much hurt.

Did they do this because they know? She asked herself. *But how? How did they find out?*

As she stared at Barb's body, she noticed a thin square of white paper lying close by. She moved to the next picture, and as expected, there was a close-up photo of the white piece of paper.

"What did I do?" Glen groaned. "We were just getting plugged into a church and everything. We were helping people."

Savannah looked up from the phone.

"You didn't do anything, Glen," she told him. "There was no way they could've known. We covered all our bases. I-I just don't get it."

She felt the advent of tears at the bottom of her eyelids as Glen staggered backward till his back touched the wall. He slid down the wall until he was on his haunches. Glen bowed his head. He let the sobs come. He'd just lost his Barb, and Savannah had no words to comfort him.

Savannah's eyes ran through the text repeatedly, causing her to feel lightheaded. She couldn't believe that her suspicions had been right all this while.

The text read:

My sweet Savannah, I admire your tenacity and willingness to help the people you have. I knew you were special. All the other families have been eliminated as they should have been. I've been thorough in making sure all loose ends have been taken care of. Glen is the last person left, and I assure you he will be disposed of soon enough. Don't try to save him; it's too late. His death is slow but effective.

My sweet Savannah, I'm not mad at you. Meet me in my office. I believe your future is bright, very bright.

Gregory R. Garner

3

He knows, Savannah thought. *I can't believe he knows.*

All this time, all she'd had were speculations. Seeing those words written in that note alongside the corpse of one of the people she'd helped save filled her with helplessness. She felt like a toy, a marionette puppet. And all this while the boss was controlling her strings. He relaxed his grip, fed her the illusion that she was succeeding in her attempt to thwart Death and save the innocent. She'd been putting her neck on the line, thinking she was taking risks and, in doing so, redeeming herself from the damnation she'd consigned herself to.

He'd known all this while, and he was what – just toying with me? It's all a game to him. How did he know about all of them? That's not possible.

She looked up from the photo on the phone and met Glen's eyes. The tears continued to flow, and each one felt like daggers cutting through Savannah's heart. Glen looked like a cornered animal, very well aware that its time as a living thing was severely limited. Savannah knew that look very well. She'd seen it on the faces of plenty of people before, people she couldn't save.

Seeing Glen so helpless seemed to be the magic spell Savannah needed. It broke her from her self-absorption. She'd gone out of her way to make sure that these people were safe. Garner had known all this while, meaning it was too late for her to change her ways now. She had to continue down the path she'd chosen, no matter what it meant. Maybe she could finally be free of the living hell that had become her life. Her mind began to work now, double-time, like the processing unit of a computer. Time was not on her side, and she knew this.

"Okay, Glen, we need to work on calming down," she said. "This is a longshot, but here's what we're going to do. I have a place in…"

"Tumor," Glen interrupted. His voice carried volumes of the helplessness he felt.

"What?"

"Tumor," Glen repeated. "The man who wrote the note was right there in my home. He said I had an inoperable tumor. He said I had three days before it would take me. He's right, though. I can feel it. It's like a presence sitting right there in my head and feeding off my life. That was three days ago." Glen wiped his face and gazed at Savannah. "I'm going to our old house. It might sound odd, but I want to die there. That's the first house we bought after we were married. It just seems right, you know?"

"Come on, Glen," Savannah pleaded. "You can't just give up like this. You've got to be strong. Barb would want you to be strong. She'd want you to live."

Glen scoffed. The gesture mirrored an audible bitterness; it was the sound of a man who had given up.

"You didn't see him," he said. "Those eyes…"

The words fell off his mouth as his eyes glazed over with the memory.

Savannah stared at Glen for a few moments.

Why can't I see his aura or anything else, Savannah wondered.

It was clear that Glen had made his decision. His decision seemed to be the only peace he carried with him. Savannah looked at those hopeless, weary eyes and knew there was nothing she could do or say that would change Glen's mind. Besides, he was right. If all the others were already taken care of, Glen was merely the messenger sent to get Savannah's attention.

Savannah couldn't help but wonder how something like that could happen? What kind of man has the power to inflict a tumor on someone? Other than what she'd heard from others, Savannah knew very little about her boss. She could only imagine what he looked like because there weren't any pictures of the guy. She wasn't sure she was up to meeting someone like him, but she knew it had to happen. Someone cruel enough to head an outfit that put people to death at a set time, whether they deserved it or not, would possess eyes that reflected the state of his heart.

However, the more Savannah thought about Mr. Garner, the more she realized that she was the only one in the firm that hadn't met with him face to face. She couldn't figure out why. Everyone else, once they completed their training, would be invited to meet with Mr. Garner. He was responsible for organizing the last training session that made a new hire ready for field duty. Going to the first field mission with him was akin to receiving a certificate of approval. Yet, for some reason, she hadn't gone through any of these.

Her mind immediately flew to the note he had left beside Barb's body. He knew her. Judging from how he'd addressed her, anyone else would say that the both of them were close friends. She knew that he didn't refer to anyone else in this manner; it wasn't his style. He was known for being an intensely firm boss, not the kind of person to address someone as he had addressed her.

I can't believe he'd known all this while, she thought. *The tone in his note was clear. He's doting on me. Perhaps that's why Jeffrey reacts the way he does to me. What does he take me for?*

Suddenly, Savannah felt a stream of anger springing up from her depths. The idea of being used by someone, even if it's her boss, infuriated her.

She walked Glen to the door and gave him a tight embrace. She was aware that this was the last time they were going to see each other. It hurt her to the core that all her attempts to set things right had been futile. Tears dropped from her eyes.

"You're a good woman, Savannah," Glen said as he turned to leave. "A good, good woman, who's found herself in something evil. How you intend to get out of it, I don't know. But keep trying. Good always finds a way. I still believe that. There's something about you."

He attempted a smile, but it never got to his eyes.

Watching him walk away to his death fanned the flame of Savannah's anger. She slammed the door behind her, and she could feel the blood rushing to her face. She wasn't going down without a fight.

It's time to end this, she thought as she walked into her bedroom and began going through her closet.

"It's about time I stood up for what's right," she said out loud. "You want to see me, Mr. Garner? Don't worry. I'm coming for you."

***

The firm, the establishment Savannah worked for, was most often addressed as just that – "the firm" – by its workers. It was on the top floor of a large office building a few clicks south of Times Square. The words "Garner's Clientele" sat at its crown in neon letters. Most people assumed it was just a security firm as it advertised to be. However, the insiders knew the truth of what their services entailed.

Savannah remembered her first time here in New York. She'd moved from a relatively small town in Florida and was shocked by the level of bustle she found here. It was the exact opposite of the peace and solitude obtainable in the place she'd come from. Nevertheless, it didn't take her much time to devise a means to acclimate to the busy lifestyle of New York. Savannah thought she had found what worked for her when she agreed to work for Garner. Her uncle, who had raised her from an early age, set up the meeting with Garner's Clientele. He referred to it as a "favor owed from an old family friend". Now, as she made her way towards the firm, she realized that she never really knew her bearing in the first place.

She approached the office building from the front and looked up to where the firm sat. Garner's Clientele shone brightly into the night like the building's own private sun. She paused for a while, imagining what she'd find up there.

Suck it up and do this, she told herself. *You have a right to stand up for what you believe in.*

She tightened her overcoat around her and walked through the revolving door leading into the office building. The security guard at the front desk looked up from his magazine. Savannah smiled at him and flashed her badge, but he didn't reciprocate Savannah's smile.

"He's waiting for you," the guard mumbled, pointing to the elevator.

As soon as Savannah got into the elevator, her heart began to beat faster and harder. She began to take slow deep breaths knowing that she'd be ineffective if she didn't get a hold of herself. Her eyes followed the indicator just above the elevator's doors as it moved from one floor to the other. Finally, it reached the last floor, which was the floor where the real business took place. The elevator dinged, and the doors slid open, spitting her into a smaller version of the lobby she'd passed downstairs.

A furrow appeared on Savannah's brows the moment she walked out of the elevator. The receptionist's desk was empty. It never was empty. The kind of business they operated required a skeleton crew to be present. However, tonight was different. Savannah walked on until she reached the main work area, a massive rectangular stretch filled with cubicles that made up the workspaces. The scowl of confusion on Savannah's face deepened. This place was just as empty as the front. Her eyes stretched from corner to corner, end to end, and they came up with nothing. There was not a single soul around. Only a few lights were on, thus making space for shadows in most areas of the office hall.

"Well, this isn't creepy at all," Savannah said to herself. "Where in the hell is everybody?"

"They're all gone," a voice said suddenly.

Savannah startled as her eyes roamed about, trying to pierce through the shadows that clung to everything around the office. She caught movement in one of them, so she squinted and began taking small steps backward.

"Don't be afraid," the voice said. "It is only me, Mr. Garner."

Just then, a tall impressionable young man walked out of the darkness in front of her. There was just enough light, so both of them were able to see each other perfectly well. Savannah stared at him for a moment with a lost look on her face. Although she had ever-increasing anger for the man, she couldn't believe that she was finally standing before him, the boss, Gregory. R. Garner. Garner's height was impossible not to notice.

He closed the distance between them in such little time that the suddenness of their closeness left Savannah short of breath. His eyes were black, blacker than night.

Glen's words replayed in her head:

You didn't see him, those eyes.

A smile grew on Garner's face as he stretched his hand out to Savannah. She was too focused on his eyes to extend her hand to meet his. Those eyes were empty, dark, uninviting, and cold.

"My sweet Savannah," Garner said with a smile on his face. "I'm glad you came in. I can imagine you have a lot of questions. You should, and I don't mind. We will get to that in time. I have one for you, though. What do you see?"

Her expression was one of confusion.

"In my eyes," Garner supplied. "You've been staring at them. I know that gentleman said something to you. He must have. I admit, they were a sweet couple. I can see why you helped them. People like them are rare to find on earth these days." He let out a laugh that made Savannah's stomach turn in knots. "But I have a job to do, Savannah. It's why I'm here. Anyway, so tell me, what do you see?"

Savannah gasped as her face flushed with shock.

"I-I-I see pain, darkness, I see…oh, my God!"

The smile on Garner's face spread until it was a maniacal grin, and then raucous laughter spilled out of his mouth. His was a laughter that was just as sinister as it was intense and self-asserting. He laughed like he knew he owned not just himself but his environment as well.

"No," he said when he finished laughing. "Not God—" he wagged his finger in front of her face for emphasis "—You know what I find funny?"

Surprisingly, Savannah couldn't feel the fear that had filled her body when she walked in there. So far, Garner had not shown any indication that he had some form of ill-will against her. And despite the fearsome reputation that preceded him, he seemed to be content on being funny, doting, and free with laughter. To Savannah, it showed someone sure of his element, someone who knew all and did as he wanted, and that fueled her with so much dislike.

"No," Savannah replied, her eyes twinkling tauntingly. "But I'm sure you're going to tell me."

Garner smiled. His lips spreading like a straight line across his square face.

"That was a rhetorical question," he said and waved his hand in the air.

At the same time, Savannah felt an invisible force knock her off the ground. She was in the air for a few seconds, traveling backward before she fell into a chair that seemed to have been positioned there for just the purpose. A grunt escaped her mouth as soon as her body fell into the chair. She shot Garner a look of surprise more than fear. For some strange reason, fear had ebbed out of her. Perhaps, because Garner had clinically murdered all the people she'd fought to save. And now there was nothing else she could do, but, like a cornered rat, fight back.

Garner began to approach her with slow, purposeful steps, his eyes never leaving her.

"I've been doing this for many years," he said. "I've met my share of atheists. They're my favorite. I show up, and when they look me in the eyes, 'Oh my God,' they say. Do you know what most of them start doing?" He leaned in next to her ear and whispered, "They start praying. Now, isn't that an odd thing? They spend their entire life denying God, but when I come along, they pray. I love letting them live longer than anyone else. Hearing them cry out to a God they don't believe in is ironic. Very ironic."

Savannah stared at him as he talked. Defiance shone from her eyes like prize medallions. Something was stirring deep within her. This tall, handsome, easily imposing man in a neat gray suit, irrespective of his possessed power, was no longer a mysterious dark specter lurking in Savannah's mind.

"Oh, my God. Oh, my God. Oh, my God. Oh my God," he kept saying with a mocking tone as he pranced around the office.

"I've waited for this moment for a long time," Garner said as he was back in front of Savannah. "I honestly didn't think I would get one like you on my team. Do you know how much damage we can do together? We were a match made in, well, not exactly heaven, but we are a match nonetheless."

"What're you talking about?" Savannah asked him.

Garner smiled.

"We are no match for each other," Savannah spat. "You're a murderer. I'm nothing like you. I was starting to make right your wrongs. How does that make us alike, you freaking sicko?"

Garner's lips twisted in a crooked smile that mirrored pleasure and amusement. He had his toy in a fixed position, and he enjoyed watching her feel that she had a choice; that she could do something if she wanted to.

"We're nothing alike, you say?" he asked.

He slipped his hands into his coat pocket and brought out a small stack of close-up photographs. With his eyes still on Savannah, he began to flick them, one after the other, onto the ground close to her. Savannah followed each photograph as they sailed through the air and landed in front of her. The photographs carried the image of dead people ranging from individuals to couples and finally, families. Savannah felt like something was clawing through her heart mercilessly. She shut her eyes tightly and hoped she could erase those photos from her memory.

"Look at them," Garner said, a smug smile on his face. "Look at them. They're all the people you killed. Look at all those children." He mimed the tiny voice of a child as he continued, "Why did you do that to us, Savannah? Why did you kill us? We had so much promise, Savannah? Why did you do this to us?"

Savannah squirmed in her chair as her face tensed up and her eyes closed tightly. She tried to block out the sound of Garner's voice and the burning effect it was having on her as he mimicked the voice of those children.

"Let me go!" Savannah screamed, unable to hold it in any longer.

"Ahh," Garner exclaimed pleasantly. "Now, there's my little tiger."

As he approached Savannah, she began to shake in her seat. She desperately wanted to get up and leave, but she couldn't move. She felt an invisible force press against her.

"Let me go!" Savannah yelled again.

She shook her head vehemently, sending her hair flying about, then she stopped. Her shoulders heaved, and her breaths came in heavy hums. She brought up her head and looked Garner in the eyes. The rush of adrenaline rushed through her veins, causing her to sweat all over. She could feel the fabric of her clothes sticking to her body.

"Let me go," she repeated. Her voice was quiet, shaky due to her heavy breathing, but not lacking in intensity.

"You think I'm going to do that?" He knelt in front of her, placing his hands on both arms of her chair, pinning her in. "Do you know who I am?"

"Yeah, you're a freaking sicko," she yelled at him. "Why do I care who you are? Oh, let me guess. It's supposed to instill a sense of fear?" Savannah managed to let out a laugh. "Because if so, it's not working."

"I didn't know about this feisty side of you," he said with an amused look on his face. "But now that I do, it makes me like you even more. You're so much more than what I thought you would be. I have to admit that I'm rarely impressed with people."

Savannah snickered and said, "Thank you, I guess? I don't think a compliment from you is something that I would—"

"Now, back to my personal history lesson," he interrupted, the look on his face growing intense. "Gregory R. Garner. That's what most people know me as today. I think it's kind of clever. When you've been around as long as I have, you get kind of bored. Yeah, that's it. Boredom." He stood up and began to pace. "Gregory R is because of what the legends, all those stupid stories, call me. Grim Reaper. Get it? G R? The last name is my favorite, though. Garner means to gather or collect. How brilliant is that? Seriously! That's the best one I've come up with ever." He looked into Savannah's eyes, and the atmosphere suddenly seemed darker. "My sweet Savannah, I am the harvester of souls, the grim reaper if you will. I am Death manifested in human form."

A self-satisfied smile adorned his face at the genius of his revelation. And then, quicker than it had come, the smile vanished. For Savannah, the expression on her face had changed, but it didn't carry the one Garner had wanted to see the most. Fear. The revelation of who he was had always brought on a sudden fear and terror in everyone else's eyes.

Savannah, on the other hand, had grown contemplative. She knew she should have been afraid. Everything about her boss said he was telling the truth. Instead of fear, she felt something new trying to claw its way out of her. She tried to wrap her mind around this feeling, but she couldn't figure out what was going on. Was she feeling the passion of making up for the families she destroyed?

Trust me, a voice within her whispered. *Find me, and I will help you fight your battles.*

Garner's revelation about his identity had helped her reflect on some things she'd noticed about her own life. Her mind brought back images from earlier that night. She thought of the family heading towards a gala to raise funds for a women's dilapidated shelter. She remembered telling Jeffrey about the dates and the aura and him not knowing what she was saying. And then it hit her.

"Oh, wait," she exclaimed with a smile on her face. "I think things are finally making sense. I knew it! I knew I was different. That's why I can see people differently than everyone else. The auras, the dates changing, the others can't see that."

Savannah looked up with newfound confidence as more things began to click into place. She studied Mr. Garner's expression for a moment. It was evident that he was slightly caught off guard.

"You knew about this, didn't you? You didn't want me to find out that I have this gift. Or did you? You wanted me for yourself. But why? I always wondered why Jeffrey never failed to mention to me how I reeked of privilege. It never made sense that I didn't have to check in with you before going out on jobs as everyone else did. I mean, and what about all the times I questioned *everything* we do here—" her eyes widened, and a smile appeared on her face. "You knew about me. You need me! Oh, this is good. Tell me, bossman, are there more people like me? Or am I the only one?"

Suddenly, she felt a fresh sensation of freedom, like the click of something releasing. It was easier for her to breathe, and the weightiness she felt before was diminishing. Without thinking about it, she went to move her arms. They moved quickly and freely.

Garner's face began to show the confusion and surprise he was feeling. Feeling she now had the upper hand, Savannah got up and straightened her pants. She had had enough of doing horrible things in Garner's name.

"What you're doing, this *job* of ruining families is evil and wicked. I'm going to make sure it stops."

Without waiting for a reply, she turned to leave.

For a moment, Garner had been rendered immobile by his surprise at what just happened. Suddenly, Garner felt a surge of strength. Now, he was watching all his carefully laid out plans about to go down the drain by a girl who thought she now possessed all the power in the world. He lashed out.

"No!" he shouted violently.

He waved his hand through the air, sending Savannah's body flying across the room. Savannah crashed through the furniture, slammed into the wall, and then fell on the floor with a yelp. Garner straightened his coat and walked towards her. He stood over her, watching as her chest rose and fell to the pace of her rapid breathing. He cocked his head to the side, and his face softened with sympathy. He crouched close to her and caressed her cheek with the back of his crooked index finger.

"I admire your passion, Savannah," Garner said. "I always have. That's why I wasn't mad about all those people you saved. But…"

He stood up and proceeded to the bookshelf standing against the wall close to where Savannah had landed. His lips moved rapidly. The sound of muttering permeated the air around them. Savannah couldn't make out what he was saying. The middle of the shelf parted to reveal a tall compartment behind it. There was a scythe lying against a purple velvet buffer, held in place with a few clamps. He grabbed it and walked back to Savannah.

"You won't win today," he said calmly. "I will make sure you never find out where this power comes from. You have no idea the power I possess. You'd be wise to walk away from all of this. I might not be able to kill you, but I assure you I will make your life a living hell." He pointed the scythe towards her and gently touched her chest, sending a jolt through her entire body.

Savannah's body collapsed to the ground.

4

Savannah's eyes flew open as she gasped simultaneously. She stared at the dark for a while, her breathing coming in short breaks because of the continuous pain in her chest. Her mind raced as she tried to make sense of where she was, how she came to be here, and what had happened.

The first thing to hit her, asides from the pain that had announced itself the moment she awoke, was her surroundings. She was lying in bed, feeling wet and cold from sweating profusely, and then wrapped with bed covers. She sat up and began to concentrate on controlling her breathing, a skill she mastered while working in the field.

As she began to focus, Savannah also observed a numbness to her left arm. She assumed the numbness was due to sleeping on her shoulder wrong. She stretched out her arms and began to work them in circular motions. No matter what she tried, nothing changed. Savannah could feel her heart rate decreasing and her thoughts becoming clearer. She also felt a wave of relief once she realized she was in her room. Savannah reached across her nightstand and turned on her lamp. To confirm that all she was having were night terrors, Savannah looked around cautiously to see if there was anything there that was out of the ordinary. She remembered going to her boss's office. She recalled the entire exchange between them both. The change of environment was just too drastic.

I had to have been dreaming, she thought. *Yeah, I was dreaming. Whew! I gotta get a hold of myself.*

Another thought hit her.

Does this mean the incident with Glen and Bard was also a dream?

She felt a rekindling of hope deep down in her heart. She wasn't a total failure after all.

As Savannah got out of bed, she couldn't help but feel like something was different. Nothing was out of place, or at least not to her groggy eyes. Instead, she observed the feeling in the room; the atmosphere was different. There was a strange, near eerie quality to the atmosphere that she had never experienced before.

Savannah began to piece together everything from the dream. To her, it seemed odd how something like that could feel so real. She remembered Garner touching her chest with the tip of his scythe; instinctively, her hand moved towards her chest and rubbed on the spot where she felt the discomfort. Immediately, she flinched as her chest flared with a radiating pain that took her breath away. Savannah pulled the bedside lamp closer with her one good arm and then parted her shirt's top buttons. An immediate fear came over her as she saw the large black mark sitting in between the rise of her breasts. The mark was a little darker than a bruise and had equally dark veins, racing out of it towards other parts of her body. More dark veins were running towards her left arm than there were going towards other parts of her body. She closed her shirt and fumbled with the buttons a bit as she tried to lock them with one hand.

Her mind was rife with seeds of fear and panic. If that whole exchange had been a dream, then it must've been a powerful and bizarre one to have had the kind of physical effects it did on her. However, what was at the forefront of her mind was getting to Glen. She felt her throat itch as she swallowed.

Some water, she thought. *Clearly, I had way too much to drink.*

She got out of bed and shuffled towards the kitchen. She flicked the lights on and almost made it to the fridge when she caught glimmers of light from the kitchen counter. She turned and then frowned. Carefully placed all over the counter were pictures, and she knew she didn't put them there.

Savannah moved closer, inspecting the array of photographs. Suddenly, her breath caught in her throat. She flung her hand to her open mouth as tears gathered quickly in her eyes. Staring up at her from atop the kitchen counter were the photos of people she'd saved. They were all dead. Lying in the center of it all were separate pictures of Barb and Glen. On Glen's photo, there was a small note:

My dear Savannah, I'd thought I could wait for him to die by the tumor I'd inflicted him with. It turns out I couldn't. Patience has never been my strong suit.

With time, you'll realize you were made for this.

The Grim Reaper.

Savannah almost puked. Her hand began to tremble, her face grew red, and the tears in her eyes swelled till they poured down her face. Gradually, her legs grew weak, causing her to drop to the ground. She couldn't hold it in anymore. She placed her head against the body of the counter and wept.

***

Savannah felt tiredness deep inside her. It was as though through crying she'd poured out her last reserve of strength and was now left empty and devoid of any more tears to shed. She stared towards the kitchen ceiling, although her gaze wasn't truly focused on anything. She felt like her heart had been forced through a mill and crushed into a fine powder. She wasn't sure if it could ever be whole again. If there was ever a rock bottom, a point of no return, then this was it. There was nothing for her to live for. If nothingness was a parallel plane like earth, heaven, or hell, Savannah was very near its threshold, and with a little push, could pass swiftly into that domain.

"God," her breath caught in her throat. She paused and swallowed before continuing. "I don't really know how this whole prayer thing works. I-I don't think I deserve to pray. If it's my time to die so I can suffer for the wrong I've done, then take me now. I can't live like this." She paused for a few moments because she felt foolish crying out to a God that she never really cared to get to know. "Can you, I don't know, if you still love me, can you please let me know you're in this? I don't understand what's going on. Give me a sign or something."

Savannah felt a rush throughout her body. Simultaneously, the room's atmosphere changed, and she felt as though she could breathe for the first time since waking up.

"I know you're out there. I guess I knew it all this time, but I've had my doubts—massive ones. I mean, how can you, the emblem of everything good, exist and watch while so many bad things happen to *great* people? I've always had trouble reconciling these things. I've tried my best to figure things out on my own. Evidently, it hasn't been enough. And I don't know what to do."

Savannah leaned forward and knelt on the kitchen floor with her head in her hands. She didn't know what to do and was merely mimicking what she had seen others do.

"God, if you're there, I need you to show me a sign. It doesn't have to be a huge sign. Something small is okay, but please leave room for no doubt."

Savannah stayed still for a few minutes. She was afraid to lift her eyes because the feeling in the room was far too intense. While it seemed ridiculous, Savannah felt like God was standing just beyond her bowed head. The feeling of unworthiness came over her. She knew she didn't deserve to be in the presence of God.

Suddenly, there was a knock on the door. Savannah jumped nervously. She listened intently, waiting for the knock, wanting to ascertain from the manner it came if it was friendly or hostile. The knock came again, a bit stronger this time.

Savannah dragged herself to her feet and cautiously moved towards the door.

"Who is it," she called out.

There was no response, so she walked closer and repeated the question. This time around, she got a reply.

"You'll get the answer to that when you open the door. I promise you we won't bite. Just please don't leave us out here too long. I think we're freaking out your neighbor."

The voice was crackly, of the kind belonging to one who was old. Savannah moved closer to the door, wondering if the voice was one of those she'd saved. It gave her a small sliver of hope.

I thought Garner had killed all of them? She asked herself.

"Have I helped you before?" she asked as she peered through the peephole. "If so, I don't recognize any of you."

"No. But you're going to help us."

Savannah was a bit thrown aback by his comment. She peeped through the peephole once more at the old man.

"What do you want?" Savannah asked. After the events that had unfolded earlier that night, she was hesitant to trust anyone, especially people she'd never seen before.

The old man cleared his throat and said, "I hate having this discussion outside. It's too sensitive."

"Well, I don't think you have much of a choice, do you," Savannah fired back.

A little frown appeared on Savannah's face as she heard the old man chuckle.

"She's good," he said. Savannah couldn't tell which of his colleagues he was addressing. "Very good. Exactly what we need."

To help ease her curiosity, Savannah poked her head out the door and glanced at both ends of the hallway. Then she withdrew her head.

"Please, if there's something I can help you with, say it now," she said. "I've kind of got a lot on my plate right now, and I doubt you'd want to take part in what I've got going on."

One of the others in the hallway, the younger man, stepped forward to speak. Savannah found herself drawn to his height. She felt a warmth come over her as she looked at him. His hair was golden, curly, full, and fluffy. Some of its curls formed fringes at his forehead.

"Actually," he began. "We can help you, and you can help us. It'll be a partnership that'll help a lot of people, not just us."

"What?" Savannah's brow furrowed. "Do any of you know how this works? You know? Knocking on someone's door? You don't speak in riddles and expect them to invite you in for tea."

The young man cocked his head to the side, shut his eyes, and dragged in a deep breath. He exhaled, and a smile came across his face.

"We actually owe you an apology," he said when he flicked his eyes open.

Now you're talking, Savannah thought.

"A lot must be going through your head right now. Why three strangers are suddenly showing up at your door must be one of them."

"We're not strangers," the lady with them said matter-of-factly.

"Well, to her we are," the man said, turning a bit in her direction. "She doesn't know what's going on. How could she?"

He turned back to Savannah, letting his eyes fall back on hers. There was a strength that lurked in those hazel eyes of his. It reeked of an innocence Savannah sought to feel, something she had lost long ago. She felt comforted by his gaze. Judging by his faint accent, Savannah assumed he was British.

"My name's Oliver. And this—" he pointed at the young woman. The lady stared at her with a straight face. "—is Isla. Lastly, this is Teacher. He's the one that has all the answers to your questions. I promise you, Savannah, we aren't here to hurt you."

Savannah looked at the old man, whose smile added to the wrinkles on his face.

"Teacher?" Savannah asked.

"Yeah, Teacher," the young man replied. "It's all we've known him as. He's kind of like the father, or maybe grandfather, of our little operation. He keeps us in line; helps us stay focused on what's right."

The old man's lips were tight and his shone with amusement. Savannah took her eyes back to Oliver.

"Look, Savannah, you've got a lot of questions in your mind—"

"Yeah," Savannah interrupted, widening her eyes. "I've got a few. Let's start with an easy one. How, may I ask, did you know my name?"

Oliver sighed and turned to look at Teacher and Isla. Isla rolled her eyes.

"O, come on, Oliver, we're here already. Out with it," she said.

"I expected this," Teacher said. "Isla is right. Out with it. We don't have much time."

"Much time for what?" Savannah asked, taking her eyes from one person to the other until it landed back on Oliver's.

"Uhm, Savannah, the thing is, we know what you do," he said.

"What?" Savannah's face reflected the fear that came over her. "What do you mean you know what I do?"

"We know you work at Garner's Clientele and that you help him reap souls."

Savannah's heart began to pound so hard she was convinced they could see it pulsating out of her chest. She took one step backward, and her hand clamped harder on the door, ready to slam it at any moment.

"He sent you here, didn't he?"

"Garner," Oliver asked, frowning a bit. "No way! Oh, please don't take that road. We're avidly against what he does. We fight against him. Listen, you have questions. I believe we can help you answer most of them." Oliver shook his head and continued, "Here comes the kind of weird part. We've been watching you, and we've been patiently waiting. If you would come with us, we could help protect you. I promise this will all make sense, but we don't have time on our side. It won't be long before he knows we showed up. I mean, assuming he doesn't know already."

"What will make sense," Savannah asked with a look of confusion. So much was going on in such little time that she couldn't just throw out her trust. She lived most of her life being cautious, just as she was taught to do.

"You're..." Oliver paused and pierced his lips together. "I don't know how else to say this. You're chosen, Savannah. That's why you're different from the people you work with. Again, we can answer all the questions about who you are and who we are, but we can't do that here. Please—"

"Wait," she interrupted, her eyes widening with the settling of realization. Savannah had been carried away by the presence of three strange people standing in front of her door that she hadn't thought to look out for the familiar things that always accompanied every human – a manifestation of the weird abilities she possessed. "You're different. I can't see your dates or – I'm so lost right now."

"We…I mean, everyone I work with is like you," Teacher said. "We see more than death dates. I'm sure you know that by now." He stepped a little further from the door, and his face went from smiling to a worried look. "We knew about you for quite a while. For a few years, we've been trying to reach out to you. The problem is that he, Mr. Garner, always interfered. We realize now that he was looking for you, Savannah. You're the answer to everything. He wanted you on his side so he wouldn't have to worry about you hurting him. This is a lot to take in. Look, you're at least one of the biggest pieces to this puzzle. Please, I need you to trust me and come with us. We have to act before he realizes what he's done."

"If you understand my situation, then you'll understand my hesitance. How do I know I can trust you?"

"Savannah, he's moving where he's not supposed to." The pain in Teacher's voice was evident. "Please do one thing for me. If you're one of us, then you'll see what we see. Look outside your window. Can you at least do that for me?"

She walked over to her balcony window and peered out. "Oh my God," she gasped. "How is that possible? Did I do this?"

"No, you didn't," Teacher's strained voice sailed across the room to where she stood rooted before the window. "Your boss did."

She looked back out the window. There was no way she could miss the enormous thick roiling cloud of darkness hanging over the majority of the city.

She turned away from the window, facing the door.

"O, my God," she muttered, a shocked expression on her face.

"He won't stop, Savannah," Teacher said. "And this time, he's got something grand planned. And you're what he needs."

"Me?"

"Yes. But like Oliver has said. We need you, and we're confident we can end this whole thing. Make no mistake, though; you also need us."

Savannah let her eyes fall on Teacher. His dark pupils shone from his wrinkled lids that were almost shut. They held strength in them, a strength close to defiance.

"Asking for your trust, Savannah, is a big thing, considering all you've gone through. But you've been chosen. You can choose to help us or stay; the ball's in your court. But if there's any part of you seeking redemption as I think, we are your only way of finding it."

Savannah felt a longing grow in her heart. She'd been surrounded by so much darkness for so long. At first, she'd thought she'd seen a window of light when she started saving people from being killed. But she discovered that Mr. Garner had supplied the window of light as a means of indulging her. Now, a door was open. It remained to see if it was a mirage or not. However, seeing three of them stand there, staring at her like she was worth more than she even knew, pushed her to grasp at that sliver of light.

"Fine," she said with a large exhale. "I'll come with you. There's something about the presence all of you carry. You're not what I'm used to seeing."

Oliver smiled.

"You've made the right choice, Savannah," he said. "I promise you."

"I just need to pack some things," Savannah said, beginning to move.

"No," Isla said imperiously.

"Excuse me, what?" Savannah halted.

Oliver sighed.

"What Isla meant to say is that we don't have time for that. And we'd prefer that things be done as quietly and unnoticeably as humanly possible."

"What does that mean," Savannah asked.

"We know your boss has eyes on this place. It might not be constant, but he's watching. We don't want him to know that you've gone, you know, to the other side—" Oliver tilted his head sharply to the side in demonstration "—until we're a safe distance away from here."

"At least there's time enough to get into more fitting clothes," she said, pointing down at the bathrobe she had on.

"Yes, of course," Oliver replied, blushing slightly. "I assume we have your permission to come in now. We'll wait for you by the door while you change."

"Please don't pack, Savannah. Just throw on some clothes. We can provide you with anything else you need," Isla said.

"Alright," Savannah replied with a small frown. "I heard you the first time."

Oliver chuckled and watched her walk away.

***

Looking at the mass of darkness from ground level was more disturbing than watching it from her apartment window. It looked angry, filled with malice and a barely restrained urge to fall and suffocate the entire city. Savannah walked among the trio as they headed towards a nondescript van parked across the street from her apartment block.

"Can I ask something, though?" Savannah pointed to the sky and asked, "What is that?"

"An aura," Isla replied. "His putrid aura."

"Whose?"

"Death's or should I say, Gregory R. Garner, CEO of Garner's Clientele."

Savannah swallowed. She turned and looked at her apartment window. She felt a twinge of sadness when she thought she would never look out that window again. However, on the positive side of things, she was comforted by the prospect of redemption. She hoped to find a way to get close to God if he would allow her to.

She began to contemplate everything they told her. There was the reference to being The Chosen One. She felt grossly inadequate. But first steps first, she had to move out of Garner's reach.

"What's wrong with your arm?" Oliver asked Savannah as he held the door open for her to go in. "I'd noticed an unnatural stiffness to it. You weren't really moving it when you were talking to us."

"Yeah, I don't know. I woke up from a terrible nightmare and couldn't move it that much without it hurting."

A puzzled look descended on Oliver's face.

"What exactly happened in this nightmare of yours," he asked.

"Why don't you tell us this on the way," Isla said flatly and got into the driver's seat.

Oliver offered Savannah an apologetic smile and shrugged.

"On the way then," he said, pointing with his head for her to step in.

She got in the van with the others. The trip was longer than expected, and everything was beginning to look different to her. It was as though her eyes were opening for the first time. Occasionally she glanced up at the evil presence that lurked overhead.

"God," Savannah whispered. "Please, don't let it be too late. I'm really sorry."

5

"Okay, now that I'm in here with you guys, can you tell me where we're headed," Savannah asked.

Savannah sat at the back of the van with Teacher. Isla sat at the wheel while Oliver sat beside her in the passenger seat. Oliver flashed her a look through the rearview mirror, though she didn't catch his gaze.

"We're heading to our base of operation," Teacher said. "Well, this is it for now. We are always on the move. It comes with the territory with what we do."

"Ohhhhh. *Our base*," Savannah repeated sarcastically. "That clears things up. Thank you."

Teacher tittered.

"We have a base around the Little Neck Bay area," he replied. "Will that suffice for now? It's easier to explain once we are there."

"I'm nowhere near satisfied. But—" Savannah paused and looked toward the front of the van. "I guess you have been okay so far. Understand, though, that I'm highly hesitant. Just because I'm here doesn't mean you're in the clear."

Suddenly, the van swerved violently to the left.

"What the heck," Savannah exclaimed, placing her hand against the glass just in time to keep from hitting the window.

"This idiot," Isla yelled out of the window at someone who had merged into her lane.

"Sorry," Oliver said, turning in his seat. "Isla doesn't usually drive. She has what you would call road rage. Teacher is usually our chauffeur, but he wasn't too keen on driving today."

"I understand, but I'd prefer *death by van accident* not be the reason why I die," Savannah shot back.

"Don't worry. You won't die. A little bruised maybe, but still in one piece," Isla snapped.

Savannah stared at the back of her head for a while before reclining into her seat.

"She might be erratic at times," Teacher chimed in. "I assure you she's one of my best. We'll get to where we're going safely—I think."

"Oh, all of you can shut it! We've got bigger things to worry about than my driving. Besides, it wasn't my fault."

"Yeah, bigger things to worry about is an understatement," Savannah said.

I wish words were all it took, she thought.

***

"Sir, we just got a message."

Mr. Garner didn't respond immediately, nor did he move from his office window. His eyes were closed, and his head slightly cocked.

"Sir," the young intern said once more. "We've received a message from—"

"I can't sense her." Mr. Garner opened his eyes and turned to face the young man standing just inside the door. "I've made my expectations perfectly clear. I know I did because I remember everything I said."

Mr. Garner sat down behind his desk and rested his head in his hands. He began to rub his temples gently and occasionally comb his fingers through his hair.

"Oh, go on then," Mr. Garner said as he looked up at the intern. "Out with it!"

"We – um – it would seem as if," the intern started to rummage through the folder he was holding. "Samuel, our watchman, has lost Mrs. Savannah. According to the building cameras, she was seen leaving with a group of people. I believe the Teacher was one of them."

The room suddenly became darker. It was as though a thick shadow was taking over any light coming from the lamps. Mr. Garner stood up, and the intern let out a yelp. Mr. Garner's eyes had turned all black, and his overall countenance had changed. A thick, eerie black mist flowed off of him like a cloak.

"Go tell *Samuel* that if he expects to—" Mr. Garner said angrily. He rolled his head like he was popping his neck. His eyes quickly became fixated on the intern. "You know what?"

Mr. Garner began to make his way toward the intern. He lifted his hand, and a scythe began to form as though it was an extension of his arm. A smile came across his face as he approached the intern. The young man began to quiver and walk backward towards the door. A tear rolled down his cheek as he fumbled with the handle.

"Don't cry," Mr. Garner said. The sound of his voice sent chills down the intern's spine. "This isn't going to hurt a bit."

He lifted the scythe and gently caressed the intern's cheek, making sure to catch the tear. Mr. Garner watched the tear trickle down the length of the blade until it had dissipated. Quickly, he swung the scythe making a violent swooshing noise in the air. The intern didn't have time to make a sound. His body fell to the ground, his eyes void of any life.

Mr. Garner walked back to his desk, pushed the intercom, and said, "Whoever's working the desk. Send someone in to clean up this mess. Oh, and find me another intern like the last one. I liked him. He was a good kid."

Death found his way back to the window. He closed his eyes and began to concentrate.

"You can hide all you want, my sweet Savannah," he said to himself. "I will always find you."

***

Savannah was surprised when they finally arrived. What they drove up to wasn't at all what she expected. Deep within the woods, sitting on a vast piece of land was an old mansion. While they drove up, Savannah observed numerous guards around the perimeter. As the van came to a stop near the entrance, several people came out to welcome them.

Oliver led her through the kitchen to get something to eat. Savannah scarfed down everything she could get her hands on. Her newfound purpose, although she didn't know what it was precisely, brought on an insatiable hunger.

Once she had a brief tour of the rest of the facility, she found her way to their nurse. While her arm was being looked at, Savannah noticed all the people that kept looking at her. For now, she tossed it up to her being the new girl.

Do they know what I did, Savannah thought to herself.

"You know, I kinda thought it was just the three of you," Savannah said to Oliver as they walked out of the nurse's office.

"What gave you that impression," Oliver asked with a chuckle.

"I don't know. Maybe it's the fact that I only saw the three of you at my door. Not only that, but nobody really told me anything either, did you?"

"Well, we're definitely more than three. As a matter of fact, we're a legitimate operation. Everyone has their role. The bible refers to Christians as the body of Christ. Well, we are kind of like a body, too. When everyone is doing their part, we are at our best. See? We are a legit operation."

"That's just it, though. An operation against what?"

Oliver stopped by a door and turned to face her. Savannah looked up at him. He had a smile on his face.

"Look, there is a lot to go over. Trust me when I say I understand. This is a lot to take in, especially given what you're walking away from. For now, can you trust me? It's probably best that we leave the answers to all your questions 'til tomorrow. What you need now is a little rest, both physically and mentally. Come tomorrow, you're going to wish you got it."

Savannah sighed. Indeed, she was tired. For the first time in a long time, Savannah felt as though she could find sleep without the aid of a bottle.

"Well, thank you for fixing the arm," she said, raising her left arm in the air.

"What'd I tell you on our way here, eh? The people at the infirmary are the best."

"I honestly thought you were joking, judging by the tone you used."

Oliver chuckled and said, "I guess I can see why you would have thought that. Admittedly, I was nervous when I met you. There's – I don't know – just something about you. Good, of course. Really good."

Savannah smiled. The happiness that glowed from Oliver was contagious; it made her feel safe, which said a lot considering she hadn't felt that way since she was a child.

"This is going to be your room," Oliver said, pointing at the door they'd stopped by. "You'll find that the room's already been refurbished. There should be plenty of clothes. Isla gave them a heads up. Let us know if they're okay. The bathroom's across the hall. I'm three doors down if – I mean – I'm sure you'll be okay. If you need anything. That's what I'm saying. I'm here if you need anything."

"Well," Savannah said, placing her hand on the doorknob, "It's goodnight for now. Hey, I'm not good at expressing my gratitude, but thank you. You've helped me a lot. It's nice."

"Oh, it's been my pleasure. Rest up. Isla will come to get you tomorrow."

"Isla?"

Oliver laughed.

"You sound like you fear her already."

"Fear her? No, it's not that. I don't know her. It's just that she doesn't seem to like me very much from the little I've seen. And she seems so stern."

"That's our Isla. I assure you she is okay. If she didn't like you, she would have made it clear with her words. Things have been tense lately. She takes what we do very seriously. I really should be leaving you to rest. I just wanted to give you an early warning."

Savannah blinked slowly and smiled.

"Thanks a lot."

As Savannah opened the door, it let out a loud creaking noise. She stole glances at both ends of the hallway, watching as Oliver stepped into his room. Savannah walked into her room, finding it quaint with modest furnishings. It had high-ceilings with long yellow walls and arched windows covered with long dark blue curtains. Savannah smiled as she looked at the bed. She couldn't remember the last time a bed looked so inviting.

As Savannah lay in bed, waiting for sleep, her mind roamed. She wondered if this was indeed the opportunity she'd been seeking all this while, her sense of purpose. Something Teacher said to her earlier that day rang through her head, something about being chosen; that sent jolts of uneasiness through her body.

"Gah," she exclaimed as she lay there staring at the ceiling. "How can I be chosen? I deserve to rot in Hell for the things I've done, for killing people. I couldn't even save them. How can I trust I won't let these people down?"

***

It was the sound of rapid knocking on the door that woke Savannah up. Before she was fully conscious and aware of what was happening, she'd been in a dream. She was watching Garner with the eye of a spectator as he tore through a pile of cabinets angrily. It looked as though he was searching for something.

Savannah kept hearing him mutter, "Where is she? Where's she? I've worked too hard for her to just up and disappear into thin air. Too hard."

Now that she was awake, she felt a strong sense of relief. She wondered if the dream meant something and if she should tell the others about it.

Just as aggressively as before, the knock came again, causing her to whip her head towards the door in an aggravated manner.

"Hold on," Savannah called out. "Why don't you just knock it off its hinges while you're at it?"

She got out of bed, hurried towards the door, and opened it just enough so her face would be visible.

"Ah," she said. A smile spread on her face. "Good morning, Isla. Sorry to yell a second ago. I'm not the nicest person in the mornings."

"A very good morning to you too, Savannah. Are you just now waking up? We wanted to give a little time to rest up given everything you've been through in the last few days."

"No, I just lay on my bed and stared at the ceiling for most of the night," Savannah replied. "Eventually, I fell asleep due to pure exhaustion. I don't know what time that was, though. I could have probably slept all day if given a chance."

"Well, it's a good thing I came to wake you up, then."

An image from the dream Savannah just had popped into her head.

Yeah, she thought. *It's a good thing.*

"I'll give you some time to freshen up," Isla said. "Say twenty minutes."

"Twenty minutes? I would like to—"

"One thing you should be very conscious of when you're here is that time flies like this," Isla snapped her fingers twice in rapid succession. "Let that be your first lesson. I'm sorry to be so abrasive. We have a lot to go over in a short amount of time. Everything you'll need is laid out for you. I'll be back in twenty minutes. You should be ready by then, please."

Savannah sighed and closed the door.

"Does she hate me or what?" she asked herself as she trundled away from the door.

Due to the excitement last night, Savannah realized she hadn't explored the contents of her room. Across from the foot of her bed was a closet door. She walked towards it and disappeared inside. Inside were more clothes than she had at her apartment.

True to her word, exactly twenty minutes later, Isla came to get Savannah. Savannah was attempting to take everything in as they walked through the hallways. For whatever reason, she didn't remember the place being as big as it seemed to be now. They passed people along the way who briefly acknowledged their presence with a stare and a brief nod.

Savannah, feeling nothing but awkwardness from the silence that reigned between Isla and herself, decided to strike up a conversation.

"You must be the queen around here," she said.

Isla turned her head briefly and then looked forward again.

"We don't operate a monarchical system here," she replied.

"Sorry. I was just trying to break the silence. Well, what do you operate around here, then?"

"Well, it's slightly hierarchical because every organization must have that if there is to be some semblance of order."

"Well, from the look of things, I'd say you three are in charge."

"Three?"

"Yes, Teacher, Oliver, and yourself."

"Well, you're almost correct."

Savannah gave her a puzzled look. Isla threw Savannah a glance, then she sighed and pursed her lips.

"Teacher's the head of this operation," she replied. "Oliver and I, we're more like, um, deputies, you understand?"

"Yeah, I do. That's kind of how we," Savannah stopped realizing that she didn't want to equate what she came from with what she was now stepping into.

Savannah and Isla finally made their way into the kitchen. It was bustling with activity, with people coming and going.

"Anything ready yet, Patricia," Isla asked.

Savannah saw a woman face them.

"Oh, Isla," the woman happily exclaimed as a smile grew on her face.

"I didn't see you come in last night," Patricia told Isla. "That was bad. You missed your meal."

"Sorry, Patricia," Isla replied. "I wasn't really that hungry."

"What have I always told you, *querida*. Food; it's as important as the rigorous training you take yourself through. Teacher will not tell you that, but he knows! You can't fight the devil without food in your stomach, you know."

"No, Patricia. We fight the devil with food in our stomach, just not the kind you're talking about. You know, man shall not live by bread alone—"

"Psh! But by every word which comes out of his mouth, yeah, yeah, yeah," Patricia said dismissively, then her eyes fell on Savannah. "Who's your *amiga*?"

"She's the new girl Teacher was talking about," Isla replied.

"That's good, that's good," Patricia said excitedly as she pulled Savannah in for a hug. "An extra mouth to feed. Well, it's rather too early. I'm still preparing breakfast, but I've baked some cakes. They're fresh from the oven. I'll get you some and milk as well. You must eat. Don't listen to this one when it comes to food," she said, facing Isla. "*Mi querida,* I should get you something as well."

"No. Not yet. I'll eat with the others. Just feed the new girl. She needs it."

Savannah would've loved to eat with the others as well if her stomach wasn't already growling loud enough for everyone to hear. Savannah looked up to see Patricia heading towards her with a plate in one hand and a glass of milk in the other. There were three cakes, slightly larger than muffins, sitting on the plate. Savannah could feel her mouth water from the sight of them.

Good God, she thought. *Am I really that hungry?*

"That might be a little much," Savannah said as she picked one of the cakes and bit into it. "Mmm! How have I never had anything this good before? I don't know if three will be enough."

"*Delicioso,* huh? They're exactly how *mi Familia* cooked them growing up. 'A small piece of heaven,' Teacher always calls them."

Savannah nodded enthusiastically as she took one more bite. Before long, she'd cleared the plate of cakes and emptied the glass of milk. She felt a slight heaviness in her stomach.

"Thank you, Patricia," she said as she got up from the chair, following Isla's cue.

Patricia had a satisfied smile on her face.

"No problems, um—" her brows furrowed. "New girl?"

"My name's Savannah," she answered as she giggled.

"Well, I'm glad you liked my cakes, Savannah. I think you can say you feel blessed."

"Yes, definitely," Savannah rubbed her stomach.

"Okay, we must leave now," Isla said, deftly putting an end to the conversation.

"Okay, *mi querida.* When the food's ready, I'll bring it over as usual."

"Thank you," Isla said. She faced Savannah. "Let's go."

They walked out of the kitchen and into the hallway.

"I'm sorry—" Savannah said as they walked "—I don't mean to be nosy or anything, but are you two related?"

"Who?"

"Patricia. The cook lady. She talked to you like you were family."

"No. I'm not Spanish. We are all family around here. All of us have sacrificed everything to be here. We will protect our family at all costs."

Savannah didn't push any further.

They got to a large double door, which Isla pushed open and walked through without slowing down. Savannah quickly followed and found herself in a spacious room. She heard a click behind her and turned to find the doors closed. She heard voices, so she turned. Sitting on chairs in front of a board were Teacher and Oliver at the extreme left of the room. Isla, who didn't bother stopping when she walked in, was already close to them.

Savannah looked around the room to see workout equipment, boxing gear, and an assortment of weapons. Savannah began to move towards the group. Oliver looked up at Isla as she approached. His face lit up in a small smile, and he said something to her.

Geez! That smile, Savannah thought. She liked the way a little smile could make his face glow. She had hardly spent any time with him, but there was this boyishness he possessed that called out to her. It spoke of innocence, of sanctity, and a sanguine detachment from the evils in the world. So badly, Savannah longed to know what that felt like.

Just then, his eyes met hers, and the smile grew wider. Savannah felt her lips spread of their own accord, replying to Oliver with a smile of her own. He got to his feet as she arrived.

"Good morning," he greeted.

Savannah was never partial to any particular accents, but she found Oliver's charming. The way he said good morning to her – eyes meeting hers and with that accent – made her feel like she was receiving an extra plate of Patricia's cakes.

"Good morning," she replied nervously.

Oliver made to speak, but Teacher got there before him.

"How's the new girl finding her new home?" Teacher asked.

"Good, so far."

"Wonderful," he said.

"You want to see wonderful, just wait till you taste Patricia's cakes," Savannah said.

"So, you've tasted Patricia's cooking," Oliver said, smiling. "I don't know what makes her cooking so good, but it's—"

"A little piece of heaven," Teacher replied.

"Yeah, that's exactly what it was! I woke up with a pang of hunger this morning. Isla seemed to know about that and took me to the kitchen."

"Yeah, Isla can be quite intuitive, sometimes," he replied.

"Sometimes? Always intuitive," Isla repeated with a smolder on her face.

"What's the problem, Isla?" Oliver asked as he rolled his eyes. "Did someone hurt your feelings?"

"No, it just seems like your compliment was slightly inadequate. My intuitiveness has gotten us out of a lot of sticky situations."

"Okay, then what would be better? Extremely perceptive and contextually comprehensive?"

"Well, seeing as I'm not a Psychological expert—"

"Hold the phone," Oliver cut her off, his eyes widening, "Are you joking? You're not?" Oliver began to laugh. "Oh! I get it. You were inserting jovial sarcasm. Wow! It's just, you know, I thought you were supposed to be the serious one."

Isla groaned and swiftly punched Oliver in the arm.

Savannah looked around. Even Teacher laughed, though his was so many decibels lower than Oliver's.

"Wait," Savannah said. "Why do I get the feeling that this doesn't happen much."

"What?" Isla asked. There was no trace of humor on her face.

A smile appeared on Savannah's face.

"You get it now, don't you?" Oliver asked.

"Yeah, I do."

"She's always so serious," he continued. "No one knows when she delves into a joke. And she's almost always so bad at it, too. That kind of makes it funnier."

"Yeah? Maybe you should buy me a book of jokes."

"Hey, that could be my gift to you for being such a gracious host," Savannah replied.

"Hahaha," Isla retorted and then looked away.

Letting out a cough to get everyone's attention, Teacher said, "That's enough laughter for now."

Oliver sighed humorously, tittered, and reclined into his chair. Savannah watched the glee on his face with a lingering smile.

"Savannah," Teacher called. "Let me formally declare on behalf of everybody how excited we are that you decided to come with us. It took a lot of trust on your part. That gives me a lot of hope for you." Teacher reached forward and grabbed her hand. "We are deeply honored, and true to our word, we're going to help you reach that place you've always yearned to reach."

Savannah stared at him for a while as though her mind was searching for what to say to him.

"What do you know that I'm trying to reach?" she asked.

"Redemption," Teacher said with a knowing smile on his face. Savannah, it's redemption. That's why you tried to rescue all those people contrary to your job description. It could have cost you your life, yet you chose to help them anyway."

Savannah's brows arched.

"You knew about that?"

"Like I said last night, we've been keeping a watchful eye over you. We had to make sure God let us know when it was time to come to you; we needed to know you were ready."

"Who exactly is 'we?' You've told me your names, but this feels heavily one-sided to me. I have nothing on you guys except your names and a location, which really isn't much to start with. Who are you guys? What do you do? And what is this place?"

Teacher stared at her for a moment. Then he adjusted himself in his chair.

"Very well then," he said. "You've taken a giant leap of faith. It's time you know what you're going to be a part of, what you were born to be."

With amazing speed for someone his age, Teacher flung his staff at her. Savannah spread her eyes wide open as the staff sailed towards her. She was only able to cross her arms in front of her face. She felt the impact of the staff on her hand.

"Ow," she exclaimed, staring at the old man with both surprise and pain. "What was that for?"

A smile split his face.

"You were able to block," he said. "It's good, it shows you're not too complacent, but you've got to learn to do more than block evil; otherwise, you won't be able to weather its full might."

Savannah narrowed her eyes and gazed at the old man. Then she looked at Oliver, whose face glowed with suppressed amusement.

"Is this funny to you?" she asked Oliver.

"I'm sorry," he said. "Somehow, it is."

Savannah scooped up the staff from the ground to fling it at Oliver, who was already trying to scamper to safety when Teacher stopped her.

"You will not use an old man's walking aid as a weapon, now will you, Savannah?"

"Need I remind you that *the old man* just hurled his walking aid at me."

Teacher chuckled.

"That's the point," he said. "*My* walking aid."

Savannah stared at him with dull disbelief and tossed him the walking aid. Teacher stretched his hand and plucked it out of the air.

That's impressive for someone his age, Savannah thought.

"Do you have some kind of superpower or something?" Savannah asked.

"Me," Teacher asked, rising from his chair. "I don't have anything that you don't have, Savannah. Actually, I dare say that you've got more, even though, you don't know it yet."

Savannah stared at him. She was trying to take everything in, but it felt like Teacher was speaking in riddles, and she wasn't privy to the punchline.

"You're stronger than all of us," Oliver answered. "That's what he's trying to say. You're The Chosen One."

Savannah felt threads of uneasiness move inside her like worms.

"Look," she said, "this talk about me being The Chosen One, and all, I'm not really comfortable with it. I mean, I can't be the only one who's *chosen.* I'm sure there's someone else capable who hasn't spilled innocent blood. I'm truly not what you want me to be. I'm sorry. And I don't know what you mean by chosen anyway."

Teacher chuckled for a few moments. Savannah stared at him in wonderment, unaware of what was said that was so funny.

"Redemption, Savannah. That's your path to God. But it's one you've got to start yourself. What's the essence of redemption if there are no sins or sinners, huh?"

"After what I've done, God wouldn't want to accept me back. I don't think that's how it works."

Teacher smiled, but his smile was also filled with sadness.

"God is ever forgiving. You'll learn that eventually." Teacher paused and looked at both Isla and Oliver. "We've all done some horrible things in our lives. Trust me when I say we aren't innocent. There is a man in the bible who used to murder anyone who was a follower of Jesus. Fast forward some time, and God personally visited him. That same murderous man is one of the main reasons why the word of God spread around the world. See? Redemption, Savannah." Teacher looked at the time and said, "You're here to train. So train. We can talk more later."

"But I have so many questions," Savannah replied as Teacher was standing up.

"I really must go now," Teacher said. "You'll be with Oliver and Isla. I believe you underwent some training before working at Garner's clientele. We'll see how well they taught you. You're going to be on more of a fast track."

Savannah watched the Teacher walk away with a slight limp as he went out the doors.

"We are a tactical operation against evil," Savannah heard Isla say. "He could have just said that."

"What," Savannah asked, turning.

Her brows arched. Isla was in a black singlet, black jogger pants, and black fingerless fighting gloves. Isla began to walk towards Savannah.

"Woah, hold up," she said, putting her hand out. "What's going on here."

"Training, Savannah," Isla replied. "Time isn't our friend. Every minute counts."

"But I'm not geared up yet."

"Well, gear up," Isla said in a do-it-already manner.

Savannah looked at Oliver. He was also in singlet and jogger pants and was punching away at a heavy bag hanging in the corner.

"How did you both change so quickly," Savannah asked herself rather than Isla.

"Time's precious, Savannah. Our enemy understands that, and you must too."

"Our enemy," Savannah asked as Isla handed her fighting gloves similar to hers.

"Yes. The Grim Reaper. You know him as…"

"Gregory R. Garner," Savannah completed, sealing the gloves' hook-and-loop fastener around her wrists.

"Yes," Isla nodded.

Without warning, she threw a jab at Savannah. Savannah's brows flew up as she bent backward, causing the jab to stop a few inches from her face.

"Ah, I see," she said when she regained her stance, "the apple doesn't really fall far from the tree, huh. Like Teacher like student. No warning, you all just make moves."

Savannah settled into a sparring stance. Both of them began to circle each other.

"You must always be on your guard, Savannah," Isla said. "Evil doesn't give you a warning before it strikes. It's been planning for hundreds of years, awaiting the perfect moment to wreck your world. I'm sure you've experienced it before."

She threw another jab and a left hook. Savannah leaned away from the jab, then swerved her head under the hook. They circled each other again.

"You've got fast reflexes," Isla said.

Savannah shrugged.

"Garner didn't let someone into the business if he thought they would bring a bad name to his business."

Isla grimaced in wry amusement. She made to throw a jab with her left hand, and, as expected, Savannah leaned away. Quickly, she put her right foot forward without breaking the flow and struck Savannah in the abdomen with a jab.

Savannah felt an explosion of pain. She doubled to the ground, groaning while Isla stood over her.

"Are you okay?" she asked.

"Yeah," Savannah groaned, looking up at her with a face decked in pain. "I wasn't expecting that. You're quick."

"Take it easy on her, Isla," Oliver yelled from the other end.

Isla and Savannah both turned and scowled at him. There was something in the way Oliver told Isla to take it easy on her that sent a spike of infuriation right up Savannah's spine. She suddenly felt like she was a child, a newbie. She sensed the same attitude she used to get from her fellow workers at Garner's Clientele; she was doted on, the boss' favorite, a bulk of her actions were indulged, and now she's The Chosen One. Savannah wasn't going to let the same thing play here. She was going to earn her place. She got to her feet.

"Do you want to rest?" Isla asked.

Savannah started to reply, but she caught the jest in Isla's tone and smiled.

"You're making jokes now," she said.

"No," Isla shrugged. "Just a question. I don't joke much."

She threw a jab. This time, Savannah parried and threw two jabs of her own. She missed, but she'd made her point. She was ready to go on the offensive.

"Attagirl," Isla said with a smile.

"How long have you been doing this," Savannah asked.

"Doing what?"

"Fighting evil."

Savannah launched forward with her left foot and threw a right jab. Isla parried the jab, but that was not all the bullets in Savannah's chamber. Quickly, as Savannah had done often during training at Garner's Clientele, she launched a left hook at Isla's abdomen. She made impact. Isla stooped, crossing both arms over her abdomen.

"Aha," Savannah yelled victoriously, lifting her arms in the air. She caught Oliver staring at her with a smile on his face. Savannah smiled. More than anything, she was glad he could see that she wasn't a charity case. Suddenly, the smile vanished from his face, and in its place stood alarm as clear as daylight. A flurry of movement before her, plucked her eyes away from Oliver to see Isla dashing towards her. Savannah threw a left jab on impulse. Isla went to the ground, the momentum of her speed propelling her forwards, then she stretched her foot and kicked Savannah's heel right from under her. Savannah hit the ground with her belly and a whimper. Isla rolled to her knees, hurried to where Savannah lay, pressed her knees into her spine, and twisted Savannah's arm behind her. Savannah cried out.

Heaving, Isla said, "Our operation has been fighting evil for hundreds of years."

"Wait, what?" Savannah said between breaths, her face cringing in pain. "How could any of you be that old?"

"No, dummy," Isla replied. "It means the operation has existed. It's been passed down from one generation to the next to ensure we always fight evil. And we've always been able to fight back, to win the battle. But now, we fear he has amassed the strength to wrap the entire world in darkness. You're the shard of light God has sent our way."

"Wait, what?"

Isla snickered and released Savannah from the pinning hold. Savannah felt an instant flush of relief. An audible sigh escaped her mouth.

"I think this is the end of the training for now," Isla said.

"But I was just getting warmed up," Savannah rolled to her back, her chest bobbing up and down.

"I like your style. We're going to put you in shape in no time," Isla said, walking towards the weights.

Savannah shut her eyes as she felt waves of fatigue roll through her body.

"God, I think she wants to kill me," she said.

"I think not," someone said with a chuckle.

Savannah opened her eyes to find Oliver bending over her, a smile on his face.

"What're you laughing at," she asked him.

"You got bloody beat. That's what I'm laughing at."

Savannah groaned with affected disgust.

"I got distracted, is all," she said.

"Distracted, eh? Distracted by what? And you raddled Isla. I'd pay good money to see that again. Nobody has ever done that. Maybe we need to work on your distractions next."

Savannah looked into his eyes. She wanted to say something, anything, but she couldn't find the words. She shook her head as to take her gaze effectively off of Oliver. After a moment, the smile on Oliver's face grew wider.

"I thought as much," he said and stretched out his hand.

"Hey, don't go having that tone with me," Savannah warned as she took his hand.

She couldn't feel his palm as the padding of their gloves stood in the way, but his grip around her hand was strong, yet not too strong to be injurious. She got to her feet, and Oliver stared at her in amusement.

"You weren't too bad," he said. "You know, you would've been a much better opponent if you hadn't gotten distracted by your small taste of victory."

No, it's not the victory, Savannah thought. *But let's agree to disagree.*

"Is this another lesson," she asked.

"Yes," Oliver said, nodding. "You're beginning to get the hang of things. The fight against darkness doesn't stop just because we've been able to light a small path. We have to do everything we can to set as many hearts ablaze for God, or the darkness will consume it again. It's time we start a forest fire in this darkness. He's becoming far too strong."

"I thought wildfires were a bad thing."

"Not in this sense. The fight against evil isn't a scuffle, Savannah. It's war. If a wildfire can win you the war, then a wildfire, it is."

The sound of hissing plucked Savannah's attention away from Oliver. She turned and saw Isla doing pull-ups and breathing through her teeth with every pull of her body.

"So serious," Savannah thought out loud.

"Yeah," Oliver agreed.

"Why's she that way, though?"

"Isla's story is a sad one. She's an immigrant who came to this country as a refugee. She had to flee her country because they were being persecuted for their Christian faith. Not everyone has it as easy as we do here in the US. Jokes are constantly made about Christianity, but all the while, our rights are slowly being stripped away. She and her family took a stand for what they believed in, and it cost some of them their lives."

The more Savannah watched Isla workout, the greater the feeling of understanding and sympathy that traveled through her mind.

"So, her parents?"

"They died. They sacrificed themselves so she could get out. We're all the family she's got now."

And an outsider like me comes in here? Savannah thought. *No wonder she's so standoffish with me.*

"We all have painful stories, Savannah," Oliver said. "That's why we're so dedicated to fighting evil. We've got to make anything evil pay. In this case, it's Death. It's taking a lot of trust on our part to bring you in here. You're the key to winning this war against evil."

Savannah looked at Oliver, at the solemnity in his eyes, invisible yet tactile. She felt waves of self-doubt wash over her.

"I don't really know about being the key to winning this thing, Oliver," she said. "I don't know how I can be. I've done so many bad things. I—you know, at one time, I actually enjoyed the work I was doing. How do I ignore things like that?"

Oliver reached out and gently grabbed her hands. Savannah stopped talking. The sudden pound of her heart couldn't allow for more words. She simply stared at him.

"His grace is sufficient, Savannah. All you have to do is ask. Look, I can't even begin to imagine what's going through your mind right now, but—" Oliver paused and looked down for a moment. "Just please trust me. The sacrifice of Jesus has to be enough. You might not get it now, but you will. God's timing is always perfect." Savannah parted her lips, about to talk, when Oliver continued, "But let's set this aside for now. Let's focus on raising the bar on your skills and abilities, shall we?"

He smiled, and happiness pooled in his eyes. Savannah felt that excitement travel between them. She felt her worries fade like they were slowly being washed away. She couldn't help but smile. This was the first time she legitimately thought about having happiness.

"More training," she replied. "Sure, let's do that."

"Good," Oliver said. Then he turned and began walking towards the workout area. Savannah couldn't seem to take her eyes off him as he walked.

Such sincerity and passion, she thought. *If only I could have a small portion of what he has.*

"Are you coming over or not," Oliver asked. "Don't worry. You won't spar with Isla. Not today."

Savannah giggled.

"What's the matter?" Oliver asked.

"Nothing, it's just your accent."

"What about my accent," Oliver asked with mock-indignation.

"Nothing, I think it's quaint. I used to read comics when I was a little girl. Your accent kinda makes me feel like I'm Batman, and you're my butler."

"Um," Oliver cocked his brow, "don't you mean Batwoman?"

"Whatever. Same thing."

He chuckled.

"If you're Batwoman," he said. "I don't mind being your butler."

Savannah could feel herself blushing.

6

"Mommy," the little girl cried out with a sniffle. "Please, wake up. Don't leave me."

"There, there," a man answered. "Shhhh. It's going to be okay. I promise she is at peace. I made sure her passing was without pain. It was her time."

The man knelt near the woman's body that was sitting in front of the coffee table. He closed his eyes and breathed in like he was smelling the familiar scent of his favorite food. There was a euphoric sound to his exhale as he opened his eyes. The deeper and more often he breathed, the darker the room seemed to become. The man slowly stood up and walked over to the ottoman, and sat down.

"Come here, sweetie," the man said calmly. "I know you're confused. Are you sad? Does this hurt? Tell me. Please, tell me how this feels."

"I—I don't want her to be gone," the little girl said between breaths as she sobbed. "Can you help her? Are you a doctor?"

"I'm not a doctor, but I do help take people's pain away." He leaned forward and gently pulled the girl into his arms. "It helps to talk about it. Tell me everything. How does this feel?"

"My heart hurts. It feels like someone is stabbing it with a big needle."

"Yes," the man exclaimed. He closed his eyes and savored the moment. "It hurts, doesn't it. Do you want me to help you? I can take away your pain. I can help with everything."

The little girl crouched a little and turned away from the man. She desperately wanted to leave, but she had nowhere to go.

"You're scaring me, mister." She tried to walk away, but the man still had a grip on her. "Please, let me go. I want to call my mamaw."

"Hey, don't be afraid," the man replied. "How would you like to see your mother again? What if I could do that for you? Would that make you feel better?"

The girl didn't say a word, she only nodded affirmingly.

The man gently grabbed her cheeks, angling her face, so she was looking into his eyes.

"This will only take a moment," the man said to her. "Do you know who I am? I'm Death. I took your mother, and now I will take you. You're just another piece on my board; I will use your deaths to stir" He stared at her for a moment longer and began to laugh. "Yes! There it is. That's my favorite part; the moment the eyes fade from life to death."

The man gently laid the girl's body next to the woman, arranging her arm to hold the young girl. He pulled out his phone and took a picture. As he looked up towards the ceiling, he lifted his arms in victory. A dark yet transparent cloak seemed to form around him. It flowed like it was continually moving.

"Nothing will stop me!" He began to dance around the bodies and laughed. "My sweet Savannah, you will join me, or I will continue to take the innocent. I will not be defeated."

He typed in a number into his phone, attached the photo, and typed out a message that said: Savannah, you're the only one who can put a stop to this.

"This will wake you up to my power; all of you will fear me. Their God," he spit on the floor as if spitting out a sour taste. "Their faith in their God will not be enough! Oh, if only I could be there to see your face when you see this picture. You might have been training for the last weeks, but I've been busy, too."

***

The mansion in the woods was a hive of activity. Everybody was prepping. They could sense the coming of darkness. Daily, more and more reports came in about mysterious deaths from all over the world. While the government was calling it a global crisis, nobody seemed to be coming up with the answers. Everyone agreed that the stench of death hung in the air like smoke, like the promise of a great fire.

It didn't take much for Savannah to get accustomed to her new way of living. She and Oliver would go out into the woods in the morning, jog, and go through an obstacle course. Shortly after a quick breakfast, she would spar with Isla. She was beginning to get better and faster and would beat Isla in most rounds.

Oliver, Isla, and Teacher continued to work with Savannah so she could identify her powers. The dates they saw floating at the top of people's heads were the expected time of their end on earth. These dates were mostly static, but only for Savannah could these dates change. Most people didn't know exactly what it all meant, as this wasn't something they had encountered before now. Teacher had his suspicions, though.

"It's the promise that there's always more to life," Teacher speculated. "That it's not predictable. We help change the timeline, and Savannah is the key to that."

The auras she saw were their live essences, a manifestation of the force inside them. Most of the time, the auras were the same. The difference was when someone's life was changing direction. Something about their auras gave her an indication that something was about to happen. Savannah learned from the others that her vision of auras changed once she started to help save people's lives instead of taking them. Teacher told her this was God's way of getting her attention, proving to her that he could and would use her if she would allow him to.

Savannah had now grown to regard the people she was with as her family. She loved going to Patricia when she could afford the time to talk and eat. But most of all, as much as she didn't want to admit it, she loved being with Oliver. It seemed as if the feelings were reciprocated because he found every reason to be around her, too. Savannah felt as if a part of her was complete when she was with him, but there was an underlying fear. Did she deserve to even think about love?

"You know, we should go again tomorrow," Oliver said as he and Savannah walked into the mansion. "I feel like you could push yourself a little harder."

"Face it, Oliver," Savannah said, still breathing heavily. "I was six whole seconds faster than you on the obstacle course. That's nothing to be ashamed of. I'll only get better and better, you know. Maybe you're the one who needs to push a little harder."

"Better and better, my arse."

Savannah tittered and fell into laughter.

"Arse," she repeated, trying to mimic Oliver's pronunciation. "Did you ever notice your accent gets worse when you get defensive?"

Oliver was immediately distracted when one of the operation agents stopped in front of them.

"Oh, hello, Marcus," Oliver greeted.

"Oliver," Marcus replied. "Good morning, Savannah. I can tell your exercise was productive. That's good."

"Yeah, you could say that. It would seem as if we are all growing by leaps and bounds."

"Good," Marcus replied. "Teacher requires your presence in the general room."

"Is it just me or the both of us," Savannah asked.

"The both of you."

Marcus turned and began walking, hands behind his back. Savannah and Oliver exchanged glances and followed behind him.

"What do you think he wants," Savannah asked Oliver. "And why is he all of a sudden so serious?"

"I don't know. People take things seriously when it comes to Teacher."

"Yeah, I guess that makes sense," Savannah said, nodding. "Grandpa checking on his kids to see if they've done their homework."

Oliver chuckled. "I don't think he'd like being referred to as 'grandpa,' but you're not wrong either."

There was a crowd in the common room, and most were standing. They were all silent, with their eyes trained on the television.

She's beautiful, Savannah thought, looking at the woman on the screen talk. She had auburn hair and pretty black eyes that hid behind the squarish lens. There was a red box on the screen below her holding words in white and block letters.

"The world is experiencing an all-time high in the number of deaths," Savannah mouthed. She listened to the woman as she continued to report the harshness of what was going on. The scene on the tv screen changed. There was a man in a suit standing close to a screen that displayed charts. At the end of the chart was a red line that spiked upwards, higher than its previous curve. Similar words floated in the air – a rise in the death toll. The tv channel changed again and again. All of them had the same story. And all of them ruled the cases as possible suicides or freak accidents.

Savannah felt a stirring inside her. Her heart hammered slowly, yet forcefully, each beat telling her something was wrong. She looked away from the television and caught Isla staring at her. There was knowledge in Isla's eyes, a knowledge that Savannah shared. And then the television went off.

Savannah and Oliver exchanged troubled glances. The air was no longer as free as it had been. It was thick now, tense, like taut muscles about to spring into action. Whispers floated like butterflies as everyone speculated what was going to happen next. An unspoken admittance hung in the air, and everyone waited for the opportune moment to say it. Or rather, for one person to voice it out.

"I would appreciate it if everyone allowed me some time in silence, please," Teacher said finally. "Isla, Oliver, and Savannah, you can stay."

The whispers ceased. Everyone focused their gaze on the old man sitting on the couch with his staff across his leg.

"I fear the time has come," Teacher continued once they were alone. "The battle against evil has always been timeless, but this, this is different. This is the battle of all battles. This is when humanity makes its last stand."

Teacher gently began to rub his temples as he whispered to himself. Oliver told Savannah a while back that Teacher wasn't a mumbling old man. Instead, he was praying. It was his way of gaining clarity.

"You've seen the news," Teacher continued. "Our enemy isn't tarrying. He's been a businessman from the start and knows to keep to business. From now on, it's war. We need to come up with a plan. I fear we've waited too long, but I also trust God's timing. Everything will work out in our favor. It has to. We can't afford to let others die."

Savannah listened as Teacher spoke. All the while, she was well aware of the drumming coming from her chest and the pulsation it caused in her ears. She could see him again, feel his presence and hear his words. He was handsome, tall, yet the danger and the malice lying underneath, she could also see.

Savannah's phone made a sound indicating she had a text.

"That's odd," Savannah said. "Everyone who would text me is in this room."

She grabbed her phone and saw the text was from an unknown number. A fearful look came across her face as she stared at the screen.

"He's found me," Savannah cried. "This is all my fault!"

Savannah collapsed to the ground and began to sob.

***

After a few hours, Savannah had finally emerged from her room. She had banished everyone and demanded nobody disturbed her until she was ready.

I'm the only one that can stop this, Savannah thought. *Why would he stop just because I joined him? This doesn't make sense.*

Savannah made her way to the front courtyard to meet the team. The four of them – Teacher, Oliver, Savannah, and Isla – sat round a drum of fire a few meters away from the foot of the stairs that led into the mansion.

"Is it wise to strike now," Isla asked. "Aren't you the one who said we should never move when emotions are running high?"

"I fear we have no choice," Teacher said, staring right through the fire. His eyes glowed like embers. "Every moment we spend waiting, the darkness grows. Garner claims more and more territories. I've never seen him move like this before. If we wait too long, we won't be able to strike. Then, all we will be able to do is defend and wait for the darkness to eat us up."

"But we have Savannah, you know, The Chosen One," Isla said, looking at Savannah. "Doesn't that give us an edge?"

Teacher pressed his lips together and gave a sigh that sounded more like a growl. Then he focused his sight on Savannah.

"Look," Savannah said. "I don't know how many more times I've got to tell you all this. This isn't some weird movie where I sprout wings and gain laser vision; I'm not chosen for anything except revenge. I can't be your precious chosen one. I've been with you for months, and I can only do the same things you do. So I see dates change. Big deal! How does that help us? What good is it seeing people the way I do while he's out there killing innocent people? Why me? Why am I the only tool that can stop this?"

"You're not a tool, Savannah," Oliver blurted out, staring at her. His expression was soft and carrying a yearning to be understood. "This is your destiny. If you continue to allow your past to hold you back, then you'll never know what God prepared for you. And yes! He's looking to prosper you, to forgive you. Your destiny is to counter the efforts of evil and deal a lasting blow. You were born to it. You've just got to hone into it."

Savannah felt frustration trickle down her like rivulets of water on a glass pane, each streak of it stripping off the confidence her training and time with them had given her and leaving her feeling distraught, guilty, and unworthy.

"I know you're not ready for this yet, Savannah," Teacher said. "But there's no other option. We'll try everything we can to make sure that this battle doesn't get to the point where it's up to you to decide our fates. It's just – I fear that ultimately it will. In all his time of coming to earth, this is the strongest Death's ever been."

"What?" Savannah cocked her brow inquisitively. "What do you mean in all his time coming to earth? How is there more that I don't know? Seriously, I can't help if I don't know what I'm fighting! Stop keeping secrets from me. I can handle the truth."

Teacher sighed. Savannah saw a deep sadness creep into his face.

"Death has walked the earth before in a human form," Isla said, stealing Savannah's eyes away from Teacher. "As a matter of fact, he's walked the earth countless times. Every 25 years, he leaves his domain to take human form on earth. He maintains that form for three years."

"But why leave his domain," Savannah asked, the shadow of incomprehension hanging over her face. "People still die when he's not on earth. Why? It doesn't make a lot of sense."

"Because he gets more gratification from being able to take the lives himself," Oliver replied. "As much as I hate to say this, I feel like he gets bored. And we don't exactly know why it has to happen every 25 years. I wish we had more answers. Instead of searching, we've always made sure to fight. Even when he's not present here, we still have to fight against his many offices worldwide. The man is a global power who's built an empire."

"He's done it for thousands of years, as far as we know, and this organization was started to try and stop him," Isla continued. "All we'd managed to do was cushion the lengths he was willing to go. We couldn't stop him completely, but we always had an unspoken agreement. If we could help people, then he would touch them. This time, however, he had a different game plan. He'd become too greedy and scaled up his game of soul reaping. We've lost some good people to him."

Savannah felt a stab of pain in her heart.

And I helped him in this business. I helped him reap those souls.

She felt a warm touch on her shoulder and turned to find Oliver's hand resting there. She looked at him, and she met his eyes, shining gold from the touch of the fire, filled with sympathy and understanding.

"We know this is the moment. You coming here was prophesied years ago. It's no coincidence that you're here, Savannah," Oliver said. "As hard as it is to believe, everything you went through happened for a purpose."

Savannah's heart began to pulse with anger. Her lips began to tremble, and her eyes teared. She sprang to her feet.

"Everything I went through," she questioned, her voice low and shrill. "Did you just say everything I went through?"

Isla and Oliver stared at her in silence.

"I killed people! How, may I ask, are all of you able to just ignore that fact? I helped Death reap souls. Souls of good people. People who deserved to live." Tears dropped from her eyes—the faces of the people's souls she'd taken flashed through her mind. There was Barb, Glen, and the family on their way to a gala to raise funds for a homeless woman. The faces kept coming. "They were good people. I knew that. Good people. I reaped their souls, and you speak to me about destiny. That I'm somehow destined to defeat what I was once part of? That—" her voice caught in her throat. She could feel sobs building in there. She turned and stormed back into the mansion.

Concerned, Oliver rose abruptly and started to go after her.

"Let her be, Oliver," Teacher said. "This she'll have to do alone. We need to pray that God would show up at the perfect time."

Oliver watched Savannah disappear out of the reach of the fire. A mask of pain lay over his face. His heart yearned to be with Savannah, to walk after her, comfort her, and assure her that everything was okay. He'd stared at the darkness for a while before he turned and walked back to his seat.

"What now," Isla asked.

"As I said, we pray," Teacher replied. "For ourselves. And for her."

***

Garner's Clientele was teeming with activity. None of the workers had encountered this intensity of work since they started with the company. They almost worked round the clock now, with very little time for themselves. Nevertheless, they didn't question the boss. After all, he'd given them hefty bonuses for the extra time they put in.

Garner stood facing the glass wall in his office. His back was ramrod straight, one hand in his pocket, while the other held a bottle of dark red wine. His eyes fell on the city of New York sprawling on the ground below him.

Mine, he thought. *I have gained dominion over you and have started with other parts of the world. I can't be stopped. Soon, you'll all be mine. Run and hide, little mouse. Run and hide. You can't defeat me.*

He chuckled out loud. Just then, he heard a knock on the door.

"Come in," he said, without turning away from the wall.

Albert pushed the door in and walked in briskly.

"Good evening, boss," Albert greeted.

"Good evening, indeed," the boss replied, his voice tainted with slight amusement. "What news do you bring?"

"I bring news about the agency you asked us to be on the watch for, sir."

"And what about them?"

"Well, our scouts detected a routine of organized movements through the city. I think they're checking us out before they make a move. It's just like you said they would, sir."

"Hmm," Garner brought the glass of wine to his lips and drank. He took the cup away, leaving a smear of the wine at the top of his lips. He ran his tongue over the spot, wiping the smear off.

"What about her? What about Savannah?" Garner asked. "Anything about her?"

"Nothing, boss."

"So, she's still with them, huh," he mused. "Hiding. Well, it's time to up our game. Come, Albert, we must send a message to our enemies, immediately."

I need her, he thought. *I really need her. I can't have influenced her life only to have her fall into the hands of the people who seek to thwart my dominance. Never. I will end them all!*

7

The trees ran past Savannah like they were fluid and seamless, like the wind that brushed against her face. She hopped from rock to rock, breathing slowly out of slightly parted lips to conserve the burn of energy she felt within. She felt beads of wetness run down her back, tickling her like a needless distraction. Her face dripped with sweat, which frequently found its way into the corners of her lips. She spat them out and continued her work. The red light of the setting sun pierced through the cover of trees, bathing her only for a moment before she ran past it again.

She'd given herself over to working out since they started carrying out field operations towards thwarting Death's plans. She hadn't gone on any of them yet. Teacher advised that she remain behind to train.

"Training is more than physical," Teacher would tell her. "You must work on your mind. Forgive yourself and allow healing. Savannah, only God can give you the peace you're looking for."

Forgiving herself wasn't something she could grasp. The burden was hers to carry, no matter how heavy it was. Being around this team and seeing their peace, made her hunger for whatever it was they had. She needed to try to connect to God so she could realize her purpose as The Chosen One. She didn't know how to begin that journey, but she knew how to train her physical body.

Deep down inside her, as she ran through the rocky, uneven terrain in the woods, Savannah felt that she didn't want to be part of their salvage operation. She didn't think she'd have the fortitude to go through with what needed to be done. Seeing old colleagues wasn't something she was confident she could endure. She knew the damage some of them had caused, the families they had also destroyed. The heavy burdens she carried were blatant accusations blaming her for trying to find forgiveness when she had a long list of the dead to her name.

The muscles on Savannah's jaw twitched as her face grew stern. Her neck muscles stretched, her biceps grew taut, and her legs pumped faster. She hopped from place to place, employing on-the-spot calculation and execution. And then she burst out of the woods into the compound of low grass carrying the mansion. She slowed to a stop and stooped, supporting her upper body with her palms on her knee cap. She drew ragged breaths and rose to face the mansion. Its exterior stared back at her with an emptiness. Most of the people who resided at the base were being called to action. Everyone was playing their part to thwart Death's greedy harvest of souls. Savannah had watched them prepare earlier, and she felt a great sense of guilt.

Savannah remembered watching Oliver's tall, simple figure and the passion on his face as he moved through the agents, spitting orders and allocating assignments to each of the units. The zeal on his face Savannah found boyish in that it was pristine and devoid of any doubt and pessimism. But it made her smile, made her long for him to be close to her so she could feel what he felt. A couple of units were put in charge of publicity campaigns that decried suicide and told people to live more carefully to prevent death in general. They were spreading a message of hope, something Oliver said everyone needed during these dark times. Unfortunately, people didn't listen to publicity campaigns as much as Teacher would have them.

"But it's not all of them," he said. "It may be minimal but we need every number if we're to thwart Death's intent. One life saved is better than nothing. We will thank God for allowing just one to live. We've done our job."

Oliver had advised that they leave a handful of people behind at the mansion so that she wasn't entirely alone. Savannah, on the other hand, felt a stab of hesitation and a twinge of guilt. She felt like she was working under Mr. Garner again, what with the special allowances and consideration. So she'd told Oliver no. It was enough that she wasn't going to be part of the mission; she didn't need to stop others from going as well.

"Savannah, you don't understand how bad I would—"

"It's the right thing to do," she interrupted, holding up her hand to quiet him.

Savannah stood up and began to walk towards the mansion. Her eyes took in its tall faded white exterior, and she asked herself how the mansion had managed to stand here for as long as it had. Oliver had told her that the operation's first leader had donated the mansion a little more than 50 years ago.

The more she looked around, the more she realized how many memories she had made while here. They were good memories. Savannah couldn't help but smile because she realized most of her memories had a lot to do with Oliver. She felt like a schoolgirl with a crush but she knew it couldn't go anywhere.

The topic of discussion many times had to do with faith, hope, redemption, forgiveness, and love. She had trouble wrapping her mind around everything but deep down she loved listening to it. It wasn't just because it was coming from Oliver either. Something within her felt slightly at peace, like things could possibly be okay.

Now that Savannah thought of these things, she wondered if the faith she lacked was faith in herself. It seemed simple to her: have faith and you can walk into your place as The Chosen One and save the world from this darkness. It seemed so simple, but she could taste the lingering bitterness underneath.

She was just almost to the door when she heard a mechanical whir. She came to a halt and frowned. She craned her neck to the left and tried to listen to the sound and where it was coming from. The more she listened, the louder it became. Coming over the treeline was a helicopter. It was soon hanging over the compound with black ropes falling from its open door. The helicopter was black.

Teacher never told me they owned a helicopter, she thought.

With alarm bells going off in her head, Savannah quickly withdrew behind one of the colossal pillars at the front. She peeked out to find two men shimmying down the rope with a stretcher in their hands. They touched the ground, turned their heads around like they were searching for something, and then began to approach. Savannah couldn't hear anything other than the whirring of the rotor's blades. The closer the men approached, the more details she could make out of their black uniforms. She narrowed her eyes, picking out the curly wire running to their ears.

Radio, Savannah thought.

Then her eyes fell on the gold label on their uniforms – GC – and her heart quickened. She'd know those initials anywhere — Garner's Clientele.

No! Savannah's mind was racing, and she was overcome with fear. *These are Garner's men. What're they doing here? I thought they didn't know where this place was.*

They kept coming closer, so Savannah withdrew her head. Her heart was racing. She clenched her fists together, willing her nerves to slow down. The men walked past her and moved towards the door. She remained rooted to the spot, her eyes trained on them. With a casual movement, her eyes fell on the thing they dropped at the door. It became immediately apparent what they were doing here. She could feel the tears welling up.

"Marcus," she whispered, her eyes never leaving the still body the men dropped at the doorstep.

Savannah's legs kicked off the column propelling her forward with lightning speed. She was fast, governed only by the fuel of her anger. The man on the left had just turned when she delivered a cross-kick to the center of his face. He felt a crunch in his nose as the momentum of the kick pushed him to the ground. Savannah didn't have that much luck repeating the same move on the next person. She'd used her element of surprise on the other guy.

Seeing her move towards him, he grabbed her arm as she swung and tried to twist it. Savannah turned quickly under his arm, preventing his twisting motion. He tried again, and she repeated the move. Garner's man smiled, then he pulled Savannah in.

"You're not as strong as you thought you were," the man whispered in her ear as he held her close. "And to think, you're supposed to be a legend."

The man's laughter echoed as Savannah attempted to break loose. Seeing that his grip got tighter, She did the only thing that made sense at the moment; she bit down on his arm as hard as she could. With a scream and a barrage of curse words, he released her from his grip. Savannah tried to run, but she remembered Marcus' body laying there on the ground.

As Savannah turned to approach Marcus, she saw the man running at her in full stride. At the last second, he dipped his head and headbutted her in the sternum. She felt a blast of blinding pain and saw white lights floating about. She suddenly felt the hardness of the ground behind her back. She opened her eyes, and they swam as she tried to gather her bearings. She blinked rapidly as she groped around, trying to get up. There was an eruption of pain in her stomach as she received a kick.

The other guy on the ground finally stood up and groaned. Breathing in was difficult, what with all the blood coagulating in his nostrils. He put his fingers to his nose and raised them to eye level.

"She broke my nose," he growled.

He heard continuous grunting and sharp cries and looked up to find his colleague kicking the girl nonstop.

"No, no, no, no," he exclaimed. He ran to his colleague, wrapped his arms around his waist from the back, and pulled him away from Savannah. She continued to lay on the ground as she gasped for breath.

"What's the matter with you, man," the man with the broken nose asked. "The directive was clear, you idiot. Don't kill the girl. That came directly from the boss. Are you insane? You know he'll know! Do you seriously want to take that kind of risk?"

His colleague stared at him, his shoulders heaving. He could tell from his flaring nostrils, wide eyes, and clenched lips that he was furious. But furious was no excuse for defying the boss' orders.

"Come on, man," he told him. "I understand being angry, but there's going to be plenty of people to take your frustration out on. Just be patient. We've delivered our message. Let's get outta here. Besides, it's not like she even touched you. I'm the one with the broken nose."

"It's an improvement if you ask me," Savannah mumbled while trying to catch her breath.

The two men walked back towards the helicopter, leaving Savannah groaning and rolling. They shimmied back up the ropes and into the helicopter. They pulled up the ropes, and the helicopter flew away. Soon, all that was left was the sound of Savannah's groaning as she looked at Marcus' unnatural stillness at the doorstep.

***

Savannah wasn't sure how much time had elapsed since the men left. Judging by the horizon, an hour or more had passed. She raised her head and looked around and was met with silence. Nobody had returned yet, which Savannah found surprising. Usually, Teacher, Oliver, and Isla were the first to return when everyone had gone out. Savannah looked towards the door and saw a long patch of dark red lying at the doorstep. She studied it for a bit before her face lit up with recognition. The memories of the helicopter and the men – workers from Garner's Clientele – came back to her.

"Marcus," she called. "Marcus, please tell me you can hear me!"

She got up and felt slight burning sensations on her body. She raised her top to find multiple discolorations on her skin. She was glad that they were bruises and no broken bones or dislocations. She moved towards Marcus' body and knelt beside him.

"Marcus," she called out once again, looking at his face.

Drained of all color was the man lying before her. His face was covered with dried blood, scrapes, and bruises. She touched his hand, then gasped and recoiled at the familiar feeling. Her eyes were wide open.

"God, please don't let this be happening," she muttered. "He has to be okay."

Savannah stooped over Marcus and placed her cheek to his nose. There was no gentle caress of breath from his nose. Then she checked for his pulse. She felt only cold skin. Marcus was dead.

Tears dropped from Savannah's eyes and landed on his black shirt. She felt pain inside, like there was a lesion in her chest.

"Oh, Marcus," she whispered. "I'm sorry. I'm so sorry!"

Just then, her eyes fell on something rather odd on his shirt. There was a bump right above where his heart would be. She ran her fingers over it and frowned. It was smooth, rectangle, and was somewhat hard.

She unbuttoned Marcus' shirt to find something taped to his chest. She peeled it off, and then something black slid off his body and clattered to the ground. In the darkness of the night sky, she could see a small darker rectangular patch on the ground. She picked it up, realizing it was a thumb drive with the words "watch me" on it.

Overcome by curiosity, she stepped over Marcus' body and went into the mansion. Inside, she flicked on the lights and opened her palm. The sleek black body of a flash drive stared back at her.

What's on it, she wondered.

She flipped it over, and her heartbeat quickened. Written on the other side was her name, verifying this was meant for her eyes. She sat at one of the computers in the common room, put in the password, and stuck the drive into a USB port. Then she waited with bated breath.

The flash drive was empty save for a video file titled "Click Me."

She double-clicked on it, and the video player filled the screen. The video started playing, revealing an office with a glass wall that showed the sky outside filled with stormy clouds. Suddenly a face filled the screen. It was a dashing, amused, and familiar face.

"Hello, Savannah," the man on the screen said. "I know. You missed me, right? I've heard that absence makes the heart grow fonder."

"Gregory Garner," Savannah said while staring at the image on the screen. "I'm coming for you!"

8

Savannah was in that place where she'd found herself more often in life – at the nadir of hope. She sat dejected at the foot of her bed, taking swig after swig from a bottle of brandy. This was the first time she'd had a drink since coming to train with Teacher. Her hair was in disarray, and her face was wet and clammy. She sniffled now and then as the tears rolled freely. Savannah's mind was a boiling pool of pain full of dreadful thoughts. Playing on a loop in her mind was Garner's video message. She could still see him, his pleasant smile, the twinkle of mischief in his eyes.

"My Savannah," he'd said. "I know you think you're on your way to redemption; that you can make a difference; that you can oppose me. How's that working out for you, huh?"

His chuckle sent a cold shiver down Savannah's spine.

"Listen, Savannah. It's about time you stopped being selfish. Surrender, and no one else will be hurt. Isn't that what this is all about? Saving lives? Making amends?" Garner's look intensified as he leaned into the camera, his face taking up most of the screen. "I will kill the people you've grown to love. Today it's one, and tomorrow it's another, then another. You should know my history fairly well at this point. You know I don't make deals, and I sure as hell don't lose. Refuse my request yet again, and I'll take out everyone you love one by one. Death is my domain. It's my right. I will do it!"

Savannah saw Marcus' pale dead face and the bloodied faces of others she'd killed or watched get killed. She clutched a piece of paper tightly in her hand and gulped some more brandy.

Suddenly, she heard a knock on the door. She lifted her eyes lazily to the door. The knock came again.

"Come in," she drawled. "By all means, come in and give me whatever stupid pep talk you feel like giving."

The door swung inwards, and Oliver stepped in. He wrinkled his nose at the stench of the brandy in the air but straightened it quickly to avoid offending Savannah.

"I figured you'd heard about Marcus," he said. "I just wanted to make sure you're okay."

Savannah sniffled and gulped from the bottle. Oliver walked over to her, his face dripping with concern, and grabbed her hand.

"You need to stop with the drinking, Savannah," he pleaded. "I understand you're in pain. We all are. But I assure you, drowning your pain is only going to make things worse. Trust me. That was my vice at one time, too. So, I understand."

"Do you," Savannah snapped. "Do you?"

She stared him in the eyes for a few moments. She then pulled her hand from his grasp and took another swig from the bottle. The look on her face indicated that she did so out of spite.

"You need to show strength, Savannah," Oliver said. "Marcus' death has devastated a lot of us, and they all look up to you now. I know that must be scary, but they need you. You need to find strength in this hour of weakness and darkness. We can help you find whatever it is you're looking for."

"Oh! Let me guess," Savannah scoffed. "Because I'm The Chosen One."

Oliver looked at her, mildly shocked. She had never talked like this to him. Savannah threw her head back and laughed. She pushed the paper in her hands into Oliver's chest. His eyes went from her face to the paper lying against his chest. He brought the paper to his face, and his eyes ran down a list of names.

"What're these," he asked, his brows cocked.

"That, my dear Oliver, is why I can't keep doing this. You say I'm special, and I laugh. You say I'm The Chosen One, and I laugh some more. How can I be all that you've said I am when I've ruined these families? When I killed all of them?"

Oliver stared at her, unable to muster words.

Savannah smiled.

"I thought as much," she said as she lifted the bottle to her lips.

"Look," Oliver said as he put his hand on the bottle so he could lower it. "Please, try and hear me out."

Despite everything Savannah did to mock the situation, Oliver seemed to be more inspired. He glanced at the names and, for whatever reason, didn't seem to be intimidated.

"This is why you need to do this," Oliver said as he looked Savannah in the eyes. "These families are why you need to devote yourself to the cause. They need you to avenge their deaths. You're called to—"

"Oh, shut up," Savannah yelled out.

Oliver stared at her and sighed.

"Leave me," Savannah said.

"What?"

"I said get out," she screamed. "Get the hell out!"

Oliver looked at her for a moment, but Savannah had turned herself away from him. He let the list of names fall and walked briskly out of her room. Savannah's shoulders shook as she cried. Slowly, every ounce of strength left her as she sobbed.

***

It was night time the following day, and Savannah was in her room putting on clothes hastily. She heard the bustle of everyone leaving. While she didn't care to see anyone off, she'd overheard Oliver and Isla instruct some people to stay behind for her sake. She'd stayed in her room most of the day, wreathed in despair. The constant image of Garner's face with that taunting smile and his warning haunted Savannah continuously.

Savannah spent a long while thinking of everything leading up to this moment. Everything pointed to what she thought was the right decision. She'd chosen a path, and there was nothing else she could do. Savannah had tried to fight Death by doing all the training she thought she needed to do. Teacher had given her hope, yet, in everything she'd done, Death still came out dealing the winning card.

"There's no use," she whispered, as she zipped up her hoodie. "Why keep trying to stop the inevitable?"

She walked out of her bedroom and almost bumped into one of the people that Oliver and Isla had asked to stay behind. She looked up to see a young man with ruffled brown hair whom she'd always seen do the driving.

"I'm so sorry, ma'am," he apologized.

"I'm sorry as well," Savannah said.

Damn, she thought. She couldn't believe how hoarse her voice had gone. The man bowed slightly and made to turn when a thought dropped into Savannah's head.

"Hold on a sec," she said. "I think you can help me with something."

"Anything," the man replied enthusiastically.

"You seem to do most of the driving around here. I need you to drive me somewhere. Can you do that for me?"

"Yeah," he reached into his pocket, "I'd have to call the others and inform them, though. As long as they say it's cool then—"

"No," Savannah objected quickly, too quickly.

The man gave her a puzzled look. To salvage the situation, Savannah affected laughter.

"Sorry, I didn't mean to startle you. It's just I kinda would like not to raise too many alarms, you know? I'm trying to break a pattern." Savannah furrowed her eyebrows, attempting to look apologetic. "I-I know I've been a burden on everyone. You don't have to deny it. Trust me! I can see it. I want to make it right. Think about it. They're busy trying to stop Death, right? Well, it just doesn't seem right to distract them while they're doing – I don't know – whatever it is they're doing."

The man spread his lips and nodded thoughtfully.

"You're right," he said, pulling his hands out of his pocket. "Yeah! You're absolutely right. When do you want to go?"

"Right now, if that's not too much to ask."

On their way through the busy streets of New York, Savannah was quite surprised by the level of activity she saw. Everything appeared to be quite normal. Everyone went about their business as though a dark broiling presence didn't hang over their city, as though Death were not trying to eradicate the lot of them.

Well, it doesn't matter, she thought. *I'm going to end it.*

The closer they got to their destination, the more Savannah began to think about her new family. Images of Oliver flitted through her mind. She thought about their last encounter and how she wanted him to hold her hand forever. Savannah then thought about Isla, Teacher, and everyone else fighting against Death. All these people were her new family, even if she felt like she didn't belong.

None of you have to die, she thought. *It's my life for theirs.*

Savannah looked into the sky, at the edges of the looming dark presence where there were still twinkling stars. She felt the clog of emotions in her chest ease with the appreciation of the beauty lying outside the boiling darkness. The beauty reminded her just how helpless she was. She shut her eyes tight, and she whispered words she couldn't bring herself to say until now.

"God, I don't know how this whole prayer thing works for people like me." Savannah paused at the thought of asking God, or anyone, to forgive her for what she'd done. "If you're there and still care to listen to me, then please forgive me. Please give me the strength to follow through with this. Please? I can't watch more people die. I'm done. I'm begging you! Help me!"

She felt the car slow, and then she opened her eyes. The moment she looked through the window, she frowned. The car stopped in front of a building, and the frown on Savannah's face deepened.

"Hey," she said, tapping the young man on the shoulder. "What's going on? Where did you take me? This isn't where I asked you to go. You do understand we're pressed for time, don't you? "

"I'm sorry, ma'am," the man said, staring straight ahead. "This is where they told me to bring you if you chose to leave when everyone was gone. Please don't be upset with me. I had to listen to what they said."

Just then, Oliver and Isla walked out of the building. Savannah sighed and leaned into the seat.

"Great," she said. "Just freaking great."

Savannah got out of the car and began to walk away from Oliver and Isla. She felt Isla's hand grab her arm as she turned around.

"Let me go, Isla!"

"I will not! We need you. Teacher said you would be here. I don't know how he knew, but he was right. Here you are. That has to mean something."

"Yeah," Savannah blurted out sarcastically. "It means I can't even go anywhere on my own."

"Please, come inside," Oliver said. "I promise we will work through this. I'm – we're here for you."

Once everyone was inside, Savannah sat in a chair against the wall of the room. Oliver knelt before her with his hand clasping hers. Savannah's face bore the heaviness of her grief. Staring back at her were the loving eyes of Oliver, full of affection and concern. Teacher and Isla sat in chairs opposite her.

"I don't think I can do this, guys," Savannah lamented. "I've tried. Believe me, I have. I'm not worthy. No matter how I look at it, that fact still remains. I deserve to die instead of letting all of you fight for me. I'm just not worthy."

"That's what he wants you to feel, Savannah," Isla said. "Don't you get it? Death wants you to feel this way. That's been his mission since before you even knew he existed."

"You should listen to her," Teacher said, "She's right, and you know it."

"But I killed people," Savannah said. "Lots of people. Children. How can I still carry the mantle of The Chosen One? Why are you still trying to convince me that God could still love me?"

"I can't imagine how heavy it must feel," Oliver said, his voice weighed by emotion. "What you're failing to see is that God already equipped you. All you have to do is accept it."

Savannah started to speak, but Oliver placed a finger against her lips. He stared into her eyes. Savannah felt the warmth of his palm running over her hands. His presence, the way he held her gaze, kept her from spiraling into despair.

"Savannah, instead of asking you to trust me, I am going to do something different. I want you to trust that God knows exactly what he's doing." Savannah let out an audible scoff as he continued, "Have you read the bible at all? Are you familiar with David or Paul?"

"No," Savannah said. "I never actually believed any of it. I'm regretting that right about now."

"Don't worry," Oliver replied. "I'll give you a quick history lesson. David was better known as King David. It's said that he was a man after God's own heart. David started lusting, hooked up with a married woman, found out she was pregnant and killed her husband. Then there's Paul. He was infamous for killing people who were followers of Jesus. God ended up using him to be one of the biggest reasons for the church spreading to what it is today."

Savannah watched as the aura around Oliver began to grow brighter and brighter. She couldn't help but think it looked like a robe of pure love and peace had wrapped itself around him; it was flowing from him.

"This isn't one of those moments, Oliver. You can't just wipe away everything I did with a couple of stories or with some super love kind of crap. That's not how this works, but I wouldn't expect you to understand."

"Savannah, I love you!" Oliver blurted out.

A look of shock came across everyone's faces as silence filled the room. The chair Isla was sitting in broke the silence as she awkwardly shifted in the chair. A screen of tears formed over Oliver's eyes, yet he didn't take them away from Savannah's face.

"Maybe this isn't the right time to tell you that, but I feel like it's a perfect time. Savannah, I think you're the most beautiful and perfect thing I've ever come across. You're literally everything I've ever wanted."

Savannah exhaled shakily.

"Please, hang with me for a moment," Oliver said. "You see, I've known for a while that I love you. This is important because I want you to see in my eyes that I would never lie to you. I would never lead you astray. You're perfect to me."

"Perfect," she questioned. Tears dropped from her eyes now.

"Yes. In every way," Oliver replied. "What's perfection without flaws, Savannah? If we weren't flawed, then there'll be no perfection, no redemption, none of that. But all these exist because God understands that we're flawed. He understands that and creates paths to bring us back to him. The fact is that He loves you far more than I do. And that boggles my mind because I'm pretty crazy about you."

Oliver sniffled, then kissed the back of Savannah's hand and locked his eyes again on hers.

"I hope I'm not too presumptuous here, but I have to believe that you've felt it too. You love me, too."

"Yes," Savannah said, nodding.

"We haven't known each other for the conventional amount of time." He chuckled. "But the love is there. Focus on that for a moment. Okay? When I say you are chosen and can do this, I mean it! You have to trust God. He'll never fail you. All you've got to do is let go of the guilt in your heart; get rid of the weight. You're holding on to it, Savannah. I know you can feel him tugging at you. God wants to help you. Aren't you looking for his help?"

Savannah stared back at those eyes, at Oliver, at the man she'd come to love. His words resounded in her mind.

God wants to help you. Aren't you looking for his help?

All the images of the people she'd killed rolled through her mind once again.

God wants to help you. Aren't you looking for his help?

She saw their faces, the vacant look in their eyes, their limp bodies devoid of the glory of their aura.

God wants to help you. Aren't you looking for his help?

Savannah's face creased; her lips trembled as the torrent of tears increased. She sniffled and lowered her head until the forehead touched Oliver's. Her shoulders spasmed as she sobbed. Isla had tears dropping from her eyes, too, as she watched everything unfold. Teacher just sat there and stared with a small smile on his face.

That's it, he thought. *That's it, girl. This is your moment of glory!*

"Let's pray," Oliver told Savannah. "Is that okay? If we pray?"

Savannah nodded.

The four of them moved together and linked their fingers, forming a circle. They spent the next few minutes walking Savannah through prayer. The atmosphere around them changed; it felt like a renewed energy, and Savannah felt supercharged.

"God has not only forgiven you," Teacher said, "but he's also got a plan for you. Moving forward, all you have to do is trust him. It won't be easy. The past is often the loudest when we are about to step into our destiny."

Savannah smiled and burst into another round of tears, but this time they were tears of joy. Savannah could feel the weight as it lifted. Her mind was becoming clearer than it had been since she was a young child.

"Thank you, Lord," Teacher said, looking up to the ceiling. "Everything is as it should be. God is good!"

They shut their eyes, and Oliver began to pray once more.

Savannah felt freedom, sweet and fresh, flow from her, unrestrained like the wind. It was like a clogged pipe suddenly becoming unclogged. Her face was plastered with a radiant smile.

But it was not to last.

Suddenly, the sound of clapping filled the room. Everyone turned to find Garner walking in, clapping enthusiastically while he laughed. A team of about ten men flanked him. Savannah recognized the man standing closest to Garner.

"Albert," she mouthed. "Oh, this isn't good."

"I guess I should say congrats," Garner said. "You three have finally done it. You've finally made my Savannah pray—" the smile on his face vanished, replaced by a malignant stare "—and that's the grandest of deceptions."

Teacher, Isla, and Oliver gradually moved in front of Savannah.

"Your dominion is almost at an end, Death," Oliver said. "You can end this now without there being any bloodshed."

Garner's evil stare suddenly morphed as he threw his head back in laughter.

"And who're you," he asked in between laughter. "The boyfriend? Listen to me, little boy. Savannah's mine! She's always been, and she always will be."

"No," Isla said firmly. "She's not yours anymore. She's not anyone's property, especially not yours."

"Awwwww," Garner cooed, making an affectionate face. "Cute little Isla, fleeing away from her country, her entire being oozing with fear as she just watched the rest of her family murdered."

Isla felt like an external valve was pumping volumes of fury into her body.

"We'd have you defeated," she growled. "Right here, right now. You know it, too!"

"Oh, the arrogance," Garner said dismissively.

Garner stared at Teacher, and then he smiled.

"Teacher," he said, spitting the name out with venom. "We meet again. I have to be honest. I didn't think you'd endure, but revenge can keep a man going when he has nothing left."

Garner laughed, and his team joined him. Savannah witnessed something she hadn't seen since joining the team. Fear. Teacher's face trembled.

"I killed your family, had them burnt alive, and let you hear their dying screams. How long has it been? Twenty-five years? You think you'll deliver the final blow you so desire?"

"No," Teacher growled. "The Chosen One will. I'm not after revenge, not anymore. I'm after justi—"

"Enough," Garner roared.

Savannah could feel a constriction grip the air. But surprisingly, she didn't feel it in her. She felt so light within that she could float above everything if she wanted to.

"The Chosen One is mine," Garner roared again. "Do you understand me? She's still obligated to fulfill her contract with me! I've planned everything so meticulously, and I won't let you bilge rats take it away from me. Men! Restrain all of them!"

Garner's men ran forward, and Garner followed behind, striding forward confidently. His eyes glowed red, and a maniacal grin on his face.

"Let's end this, shall we," he roared. His voice was guttural and resounding. "Let's see how confident you are in your God now."

Oliver, Isla, Teacher, and Savannah got into their fighting stances. Isla saw a man coming toward her. She instinctively grabbed the chair she had been sitting in and smashed it across the man's head. His body hit the floor with a loud thud. Isla reached to punch the next person, but someone dove into her from the side, taking her to the ground.

A few feet away from her, Oliver was fighting two men, delivering punches, and trying to block. Now and then, Oliver would let out a laugh as though he was enjoying the moment.

Teacher was usually slow and methodical in everything he did. Today, Teacher made his way toward Garner and did it with a passion in each step.

"Come, Teacher. Come on! Let's dance," Death roared, a devilish grin on his face. "I'd love to be the one to end your life finally."

"I'm sending you back to where you belong," Teacher said. He tugged at the knurled top of his staff, and it came off with a long blade attached to it.

Albert and Savannah squared off.

"Isn't this interesting. Once again, you have to be Daddy's girl," Albert seethed. "I'm not allowed to kill you because the boss has plans for you, but it doesn't mean I won't whoop your…"

Savannah stepped forward with her left foot, placed both hands atop Albert's shoulders, and drove her right knee into his crotch. Albert's eyes widened, and his face reddened as unimaginable pain traversed his body. He groaned and dropped to the ground when Savannah removed her hands from his shoulders. She gave him an uppercut to the jaw, sending him collapsing backward.

"Seriously! Has anyone ever told you that you talk too much," she asked and moved on.

Someone tried to throw a punch straight to Savannah's face. She grabbed his arm, dug her shoulder under it, lifted him over her, and violently threw him to the ground. Savannah dealt a hard right kick to his head, rendering him unconscious.

Savannah turned to wade further into the center of the action but stopped as though a wall hit her. Death, lashing out with his hand, telekinetically smashed Oliver and Isla against the wall. Savannah saw their faces squeeze in pain as their backs touched the wall. She saw agents rising to their feet and going in for the kill. She looked at Death, and he stared back at her with a grin on his face. Her eyes widened with horror as she saw Teacher on the ground, struggling to lift Death's foot from off his neck.

"Let him go," Savannah screamed. She felt frustration and helplessness, like plumes of smoke begin to stain her new-found liberty.

"I'm tired of playing games. You can't defeat me! One move of the hand, and they're dead. You're mine, Savannah." Death smiled widely. "You can feel it. I know you can. You're mine!"

Death pointed at Savannah, and his eyes glowed brighter with anger.

"Have you ever asked yourself how you came to work with me?"

Savannah stared at him but chose not to answer.

"I took care of you, Savannah. You'd be nothing without me. And I made sure of that. I killed off your parents like I did to Teacher's family—" he bent down to look at the old man, whose face was beginning to pale as he struggled to breathe.

"What," Savannah whispered, staggering backward as she'd just been delivered a sucker punch. She couldn't breathe. It was as though her lungs had turned to stone.

"Yes, Savannah," Death boasted as he took a bow. "That's right! I killed them. That should tell you the extent to which I went to make you mine. I'm a jealous owner, a businessman. You know this. I invested, and I expect a payout. You see? I don't lose."

Tears fell from Savannah's eyes like liquid pebbles. She heard cries and screams and turned to find Oliver and Isla under a barrage of punches and kicks. Blood was beginning to stain their clothes as the men continued. This was no merciful death. Savannah saw this now. None of them had come with any weapons. Death was keeping this brutal, cruel, slow. Her friends, her family, they would die from the pummeling of fists and kicks. Death would take them just as he'd taken her first family. What could she do? They were dying already. Death was too strong for her. And right there, teetering at the edge of hopelessness, about to give in, she heard his voice – Oliver's voice.

God wants to help you. Aren't you looking for his help?

She heard Teacher's voice:

God has not only forgiven you; he's got a plan for you.

Isla's voice:

Your hold over her is broken.

"Your hold over me is broken," Savannah repeated over and over again. With each repetition, she felt her new-found freedom edge out the despair that'd sought to claw back in.

Then she shut her eyes and breathed deeply.

Your hold over me is broken, she thought.

"My father in heaven," she whispered. "Let your will be done."

Death stared down at Teacher, whose struggle was weakening, and began to press down harder on the man's throat. Suddenly, there was a blast of light from the periphery of his vision, causing him to flinch and raise his hand over his face.

"What's this," he roared, trying to peer through his fingers and see what the source of the light was.

"What? You don't recognize it," Savannah's voice floated over to him. "It's the hand of God. It's the might of justice. This is me realizing my destiny!"

Death's eyes grew redder, and he stepped off Teacher's throat. The old man rolled off his back the moment he got free and began to cough convulsively. Death faced Savannah and bellowed, his incisors grew sharper, his muscles bulged, and his tongue forked.

"Who do you think you are," he roared. "There is no power you could ever possess that could cause me to recoil. I own you, little girl!"

The men who'd been beating Oliver and Isla watched the light that radiated from Savannah. With shocked expressions, they left Oliver and Isla breathing heavily on the ground. Their faces were a canvas of blood, bruises, and cuts.

A dark cloak engulfed Death. He stretched out his right hand, and a long scythe appeared. The side of the room he was standing on began to get darker and colder. Death let out a guttural laugh that made even his men cringe and hold their ears.

"I will not be defeated. You'll all die tonight! Enough is enough! If you don't join me, then you'll join your dead parents."

Savannah stared at Death, and she felt a righteous rage course through her. She latched on to it, let it feed her, and her feet lifted off the ground. She sailed into the air like the rising of the morning sun.

"Death," she yelled as a smile grew across her face. "Your judgment has come."

Death's laughter suddenly ceased and was replaced with anger.

"You're a child," he roared and dashed at Savannah, his jaws wide apart, forked tongue lashing out like a whip.

Savannah screamed, and the intensity of the light increased. Teacher winced and dove to the ground, peering through his hands to see Savannah holding up her hand.

"No," Savannah calmly said, stopping Death in midair. "It's over. Your time is done."

Death was suddenly engulfed by a bright light that filled the entirety of the room. Every shadow in the room dissipated within seconds. Death let out a scream that was no longer filled with rage. Instead, his screams were laced with fear. All over New York, thunder rumbled in the darkened sky, and lightning crackled. Anyone intent enough could hear the unearthly scream of Death. The light from Savannah began to tear away at Death as if burning off his flesh until nothing was left of him.

Savannah turned towards Death's men, who were all huddled together at the opposite side of the room.

"You will find a way to repay the families that have been left hurting," Savannah said as she pointed at the men. "We will find you. Now leave!"

Savannah closed her eyes and lowered to the ground as Death's men hurried away. Oliver, Isla, and Teacher made their way over to her, and they all embraced. She let out a joyous laugh.

"What was that," Isla asked. "Like, what exactly just happened?"

"It was a flood," Savannah answered. "I felt forgiven. That's the first time I ever experienced that. It was like love wrapped its arms around me. Then I looked at the three of you. My love turned into anger, but good anger. Does that make sense?"

"Yes," Teacher replied. "It makes perfect sense."

The next morning, Teacher, Isla, and a group of other agents sat outside the mansion, talking and joking under the soft glow of the rising sun. A cool breeze cruised through from the trees, adding a pleasant texture to the ambiance. Savannah sat a few feet away from the rest, a smile on her face, black hair dancing to the tune of the breeze. Her eyes were on Oliver as he stood atop the scaffolding, one among several agents giving the mansion a much-needed paint job. She heard Isla laugh, and she cocked her brows in surprise.

That's a first, she thought, and she couldn't help smiling as she watched Isla move back and forth, shaken by the turbulence of laughter, while several faces stared at her with shock.

Savannah stared at a sizable book in her office. She dug into the breast pocket of her denim shirt and brought out a photo. She opened the book and slipped the photo into a compartment made from a cellophane screen. With a permanent marker, she added names next to the picture. A radiant smile sat on her face all the while. She closed the book and stared at its cover.

"Thank you, God," she whispers. "Just – thank you!"

Those words at the middle of the book's cover stared back at her, black and bold against the book's yellow cover:

Lives Saved

Coming soon:

Be on the lookout for the third book in the series, *Feel the Music*. The short story was one that so many people loved. I look forward to you reading about Emily and what she does with her newfound power.

Seeing my short stories come to life and become their own novellas has proven to be a lot more fun than I thought it would be. I look forward to sharing more books with you in the future.

This book is the second of five that are based on short stories from my book, Ellipsis: Short Stories to Inspire the Imagination. I would love for you to read it and let me know what you think. Go to **www.robbiembowman.com** and get your free digital copy.

About the Author:

Robbie Michael resides in Shreveport, Louisiana, with his wife, who he affectionately refers to as "Wife." He is always talking about moving to Liverpool and is excepting house donations if anyone is feeling generous. Robbie and his wife have a small army of children that recently went through an unexpected expansion. The newest addition to the Bowman family is their beautiful little son, Xander Luke. For real, go look on his Instagram. There are a ton of pictures of all the cuteness.

Robbie has a love for writing and hopes to soon start sharing that passion with the next generation. There is the possibility that his book of short stories will be used in a few schools. Make sure to follow him on social media so you can keep up with everything.

Facebook: www.facebook.com/OfficialRobbieBowman

Instagram: www.instagram.com/robbie_bowman